CABIN SIX
HAS A PROBLEM

ERIN thinks she's too grown up for the girls from Cabin Six and she's found some new friends from Cabin Nine.

TRINA remembers the Cabin Nine girls from the Color War—and how mean and unfair they were.

MEGAN can't believe Erin would have anything to do with them.

SARAH thinks she can count on Erin when she needs her, but finds out Erin's new friends come first.

KATIE warns Erin about breaking the rules to impress her new friends, but Erin won't listen.

CAMP SUNNYSIDE FRIENDS #5

Looking For Trouble

Marilyn Kaye

AN AVON  CAMELOT BOOK

CAMP SUNNYSIDE FRIENDS #5: LOOKING FOR TROUBLE is an original publication of Avon Books. This work has never before appeared in book form.

AVON BOOKS
A division of
The Hearst Corporation
105 Madison Avenue
New York, New York 10016

Copyright © 1990 by Marilyn Kaye
Published by arrangement with the author
Library of Congress Catalog Card Number: 89-91924
ISBN: 0-380-75909-8
RL: 4.5

First Avon Camelot Printing: January 1990

CAMELOT TRADEMARK REG. U.S. PAT. OFF. AND IN OTHER COUNTRIES, MARCA REGISTRADA, HECHO EN U.S.A.

Printed in the U.S.A.

OPM 10 9 8 7 6 5 4 3 2 1

For Delaney and Kerianne Steele

Chapter 1

Erin Chapman stood in front of the mirror and carefully applied eyeliner. She had a supply of cotton tips close at hand in case she smudged, but she didn't need them. The black line just above her eyelashes was smooth. She stepped back and critically examined her work. Not bad for a first time, she decided.

In the reflection, she could see behind her the other cabin six girls getting ready for dinner. Katie Dillon was on her top bunk bed, making a halfhearted attempt to clean her tennis shoes. Below her, Trina Sandburg was changing her clothes. Across from them, Sarah Fine brushed her hair with one hand while turning a page in her book with the other. And Megan Lindsay was staring into space while going through the motions of tying her shoelaces.

But Erin was only dimly aware of all this activity. There was something very important on her mind. "Do you guys think I should get my hair cut?" She turned to face her cabin mates.

Sarah glanced up from her book. "Sure, if you want to."

"Short hair dries faster," Trina noted, touching her own.

"But how do you think it would look?" Erin pressed them.

Katie looked down from her bed. "Like short hair."

"Very funny," Erin retorted. "Haven't any of you guys looked at a fashion magazine lately? Short hair is very in. Which means long hair is out." She gathered her blonde hair and held it over her shoulders. "Seriously, do you think I would look good?"

"Sure," Trina said. But she was in the process of pulling a tee shirt over her head and wasn't even looking.

"Megan, what do you think?" Erin asked.

Megan blinked. "Huh?" It was obvious she'd been off on one of her usual daydreams and hadn't even been listening.

Erin rolled her eyes in exasperation. "Where have *you* been? We're talking about my hair."

2

"What about it?"

"How do you think I'd look with short hair?"

Megan stared at her blankly. "Same way you look now. Only with less hair."

Erin groaned. "Oh, forget it." She let her hair drop back down. "Honestly, you guys don't know anything about style."

Katie slapped a hand to her forehead. "Golly gee whiz, Erin, we're so terribly sorry." She fell back on her bed dramatically.

Erin gave up. She went back to the mirror and started putting on mascara. Katie climbed down from her bed and checked herself in the mirror. Then she looked at Erin's reflection more closely.

"Why are you putting all that gook on your face?"

"It's not gook. For your information, it's called makeup. I guess you've never heard of it."

Trina joined them at the mirror. "Why are you wearing makeup?"

"Because I feel like it," Erin replied. "Besides, I think it makes me look older and more sophisticated."

"It makes you look silly," Katie said bluntly. "Nobody wears makeup at camp."

Her comment didn't bother Erin. She was used to Katie. "The girls in cabin nine wear makeup."

"But they're thirteen," Katie noted. "A couple of them are even fourteen. You're only eleven."

"I'm almost twelve," Erin pointed out. "Anyway, Katie, your opinion doesn't mean much, considering the fact that you look half your age."

"Half my age? Hmm, that would make me five and a half." Katie promptly stuck a thumb in her mouth.

Trina laughed, but when she turned back to Erin her expression was serious. "I don't know if Carolyn's going to let you out of the cabin with all that makeup on."

As if on cue, their counselor emerged from her private room. "Everyone ready for dinner?"

Erin turned her head away slightly so Carolyn couldn't see her. Personally, she thought Carolyn actually might be the only person in the cabin who would understand her desire to wear makeup. After all, she was nineteen. But sometimes, she did treat the campers like children.

Erin stayed in the back of the group as Carolyn led them outside. As they headed toward the dining hall, Sarah walked alongside her. She studied Erin's face thoughtfully.

"That makeup *does* make you look older."

"Thank you," Erin said, grateful to have one person who approved.

"But you don't need it. You're pretty without makeup." Sarah sighed. "I wish I had your looks."

Erin smiled kindly. Sarah certainly wasn't ugly. But with her plain brown straight hair and her ordinary features, she wasn't beautiful either. And those glasses certainly didn't help.

"Have you ever considered getting contact lenses?"

Sarah made a face. "I hate the idea of sticking those plastic things in my eyes."

"Sometimes you have to suffer to be beautiful," Erin told her.

Sarah grinned. "Then I guess I'll never be beautiful. It's not worth suffering for." She skipped on ahead.

Erin shook her head ruefully. She should have known better. Sarah just wasn't mature enough to understand. None of the cabin six girls was.

Sadly, she pondered her situation. What was she, Erin Chapman, doing at Camp Sunnyside with these kids anyway? Just because she'd gone every year since she was eight didn't mean she had to be here now when she was almost twelve. She should have fought harder to stay home.

She wondered what the kids back home were doing right that minute. Probably having a cookout or a swimming party at someone's house. Maybe they'd dance afterwards. And her sort-of boyfriend, Alan, was probably flirting and dancing with some other girl.

And here she was, stuck at an all-girl camp with no one to flirt with. She'd just spent a half hour fussing with her hair and putting on makeup, with no one to appreciate it.

Of course, there was Bobby, at Camp Eagle just across the lake. Whenever they had activities with Eagle, like camp fires, Bobby hung around her. But having a boys' camp across the lake wasn't much comfort. It wasn't like home, where you could see boys every day.

By the time they got to the dining hall, Erin's thoughts had made her feel glum. And the sight of a huge room filled with noisy girls, running around and yelling to one another, didn't improve her mood.

They joined the line to get their trays. "What's for dinner?" Megan was hopping from one foot to the other and trying to see ahead. It was a habit Erin found particularly annoying.

"Megan, quit that. You're acting like a baby."

Megan didn't seem at all disturbed by that. "Ooh, roast beef and mashed potatoes!"

"Mashed potatoes?" Katie's eyes lit up. Erin was alarmed to see a slow grin spreading across her face.

"Katie, I hope you're not thinking what I think you're thinking."

Katie grinned. "Aw, c'mon, we haven't had a real food fight all summer."

She'd spoken too loudly. Carolyn turned around. "And you're not going to have one tonight." Then she looked past Katie, directly at Erin. "Erin, you're wearing makeup."

Erin nodded, and geared herself to defend her right to put whatever she wanted on her face. To her surprise, Carolyn didn't start scolding her.

"You might want to try lighter shades on your eyes next time. You can borrow some of mine if you like. I'll show you how to blend shadow, too."

Megan started giggling. "Hey, maybe you could start giving makeup lessons as a regular camp activity. Like arts and crafts."

Sarah giggled too as she picked up on Megan's idea. "Yeah, maybe we could get it into the daily schedule. Horseback riding, swimming, archery, and makeup."

"Why don't we just change the camp completely?" Katie suggested, laughing. "I can just see the sign now. 'Camp Sunnyside—no horses, no lake, just fashion and makeup.' "

They were teasing her. Erin felt like she had four pesty little sisters. Even Trina, who was usually pretty down-to-earth, was laughing as they continued to make jokes.

Erin set her mouth in a tight line. She wasn't about to let them get to her. She was too mature to get involved in this nonsense.

They collected their trays and went to their usual table. "Hey, did you guys hear what cabin seven did to cabin five?" Megan asked.

"No, what?" Katie asked.

"They sneaked into the cabin while everyone was at the pool and switched their tennis shoes around. So when they got back and started putting on their shoes, everyone had the wrong size. I heard it was a riot."

"That's pretty cool," Katie said with approval. "You know, we haven't played any really good pranks yet on another cabin this summer."

Carolyn gave her a warning look. "I hope you're not planning any now."

"I'm not talking about anything dangerous or mean," Katie assured her. "Just harmless pranks. The kind people laugh at."

Erin shook her head. "Pranks are so infantile, Katie."

Katie's eyebrows shot up. "You didn't think so last summer. Remember when we spread that rumor about a ghost haunting cabin three? And you put that sheet over your head and ran by their windows?"

Erin hoped she wasn't blushing at the memory. "That was a long time ago."

"It was just last summer," Sarah said.

Erin flipped her hair over her shoulder. "I was a child last summer."

Trina smiled. "What are you now? A senior citizen?"

"Speaking of senior citizens . . ." Katie murmured and looked pointedly just past Erin. Erin turned.

Some of the cabin nine girls—Maura Kingsley, Andrea Hill, and another girl—were walking toward their table with their trays.

"Double ick," Sarah muttered. Erin knew Sarah had never liked Maura, because the older girl had teased her when Sarah was chubbier.

Katie didn't like her either. They'd had real battles back when they were captains of opposing teams during color war.

Maura could be kind of mean, Erin thought. But even so, her eyes followed the girls to their table. That table had a totally different atmosphere. The girls actually seemed to be talking, not screeching or giggling. Their heads were bent close, in a confidential way, as if whatever they were talking about was important and secretive.

They looked different, too. Even in the standard Sunnyside tee shirts and shorts, they looked fashionable. One of the girls had tied her tee shirt into a knot under her midriff. Another had cut the neckline so the shirt hung just slightly over her shoulders. They wore makeup, and their hair had style. You could tell just from looking at them that they were thirteen.

Erin watched them longingly. She might be only almost twelve, but she *felt* thirteen. Those girls in cabin nine would never tease her about makeup. And she was certain they took the idea of haircuts very seriously.

Her eyes wandered back to her own cabin mates. Funny, she used to think of them as great friends. But how could she feel close to them now? She'd changed. They hadn't. They really had nothing in common anymore. Suddenly, she felt very depressed.

"Girls, could I have your attention, please?"

All heads turned toward Ms. Winkle, standing at the front of the room. Erin only half listened. It was the camp director's usual dinnertime announcements about night swims and movies on the lake and trips into Pine Ridge.

But then she heard something that grabbed her full attention. "Camp Eagle has invited us to a camp fire and cookout on Wednesday. This will be the first time this summer that we'll be visiting Eagle, so it's a special occasion."

That announcement lifted Erin's spirits. She'd see Bobby—not to mention all those other boys! Maybe they'd have dancing after the cookout. Mentally, she started planning what she'd wear.

The others seemed pleased by the news too. "Hey, maybe we can organize a softball game there," Katie suggested. "Boys against girls!"

Erin groaned. She certainly had no intention of getting sweaty and dirty when she was surrounded by boys. "Softball is kids' stuff," she muttered, but no one heard her. They were all telling Katie what a great idea that was.

She glanced over at the cabin nine table. They seemed to be talking more excitedly now.

11

They're probably making plans for the visit to Camp Eagle too, Erin thought.

And she suspected their plans had nothing whatsoever to do with softball.

Chapter 2

Erin rolled over in her bed and half opened her eyes. The moonlight illuminated the sleeping faces around her. It had to be the middle of the night. What had woken her? she wondered. Then she heard the noise—like little taps at the window by her bed. That's odd, she thought sleepily, hail in the summer.

That thought jerked her wide awake. Hail in the summer? She sat up and rubbed her eyes.

The noise continued. On the other side of the room, Trina sat up too. "What's that noise?" she asked in a whisper. Above her, Katie was stirring restlessly.

"I don't know," Erin whispered back.

Then Katie spoke from her pillow, her voice muffled. "What's going on?" At the same time, Sarah pulled herself up. "What's that rattling at the window?"

The girls all stared at one another for a second. Then, simultaneously, they all got out of their beds and hurried over to the window.

"Who are they?" Trina asked in a frightened voice.

Katie pressed her face against the glass pane. Then, something hit the window, and she jumped back. "They're boys!"

"Let me see," Erin said. She squeezed in between them and peered out. Then she gasped. "It's Bobby!"

Sure enough, Bobby was standing under their window, along with four other boys in Camp Eagle sweatshirts. They were tossing pebbles at their window.

A tingle went through Erin. Bobby, standing under her window at midnight! How romantic! She glanced furtively at Carolyn's door. Then she eased the window open.

"Hi!"

Bobby stared at her, his mouth open. "Is this *your* cabin?"

"Of course! Didn't you know that?"

Still looking dumbstruck, Bobby shook his head.

"What are you guys doing here in the middle of the night?" Katie demanded.

The boys' expressions ranged from cocky to embarrassed. Finally Bobby spoke. "It was a dare. This other cabin challenged us to sneak over here. We're supposed to bring back a, uh, . . ." Even in the darkness, Erin could see that his face was beet red.

"A what?" Erin asked.

She could barely hear him because now he was staring at the ground. "Underwear. We're supposed to bring back girls' underwear."

"This is unreal," Sarah murmured.

Katie nodded. "What a bunch of jerks."

At first, Erin bristled. How dare Katie call Bobby a jerk? On the other hand, she had to admit his request was pretty silly. And the more she thought about it, the more annoyed she felt. This was nothing but a panty raid. Bobby hadn't even planned to see her—they'd just picked cabin six by accident.

"How did you get here?" Trina asked, her eyes wide.

"We sneaked out of our cabin," one of the boys said, "and we rowed a canoe across the lake."

Trina looked shocked. "You could be in serious trouble!"

"Not unless we get caught," a boy replied smugly.

"Shh," Erin hissed. "Keep your voice down. Or you *will* get caught."

15

"And get out of here," Katie added.

"Okay, we'll go," Bobby said, "but give us something to take back, okay? Otherwise, no one will believe we got here."

Sarah put her hands on her hips. "Do they really expect us to give them a bra or something?"

"No way," Katie stated firmly.

Erin bit her lip. Then she had an idea. She hurried over to her dresser and fumbled around in a drawer. Then she ran back to the window. "Here!" And she flung a sock at them.

She stifled a giggle at the look of disappointment on their faces. Then she firmly closed the window.

"Boys." Katie groaned. "Honestly. They're all idiots."

Trina still looked appalled. "Sneaking out of their cabin—they could get sent home for that."

"Pretty dumb thing to do," Sarah agreed. She started to climb her ladder to bed, then poked her head under it. "Hey, Megan slept through all that!"

"Well, she didn't miss much," Katie said, yawning.

Erin had to agree as she climbed back into bed. Raiding a girls' camp was such a juvenile thing. And Bobby had been a part of it. She was definitely disappointed in him.

Oh well, she thought as she pulled up her covers, there was the camp fire at Eagle on Wednesday. Maybe she'd be able to find someone more mature.

The next morning, the girls filled Megan in on what she'd slept through. "Gee, I missed all the excitement!" she wailed. "Why didn't you guys wake me?"

Sarah patted her shoulder. "Megan, even when you're not sleeping, you're not really awake."

"Did you really give them a sock?" Megan asked Erin.

"Yeah. And I know they were expecting—" She stopped abruptly. Carolyn was coming out of her room.

On the way to the dining hall, Erin pulled Katie aside. "Listen, don't tell any of the other campers what happened. It might get back to Ms. Winkle, and I don't want Bobby getting into trouble. Pass it on."

Bobby might have acted like a jerk, she thought, but if Ms. Winkle found out she might notify the director at Eagle. And she didn't want Bobby sent home. Because, if she didn't meet

17

anyone else at the camp fire, she'd at least have him to flirt with.

Katie gave her a reluctant okay. Erin could tell she was dying to spread the story. But cabin six loyalties came first, and she knew the others wouldn't tell if Erin didn't want them to. It would just have to be their secret.

Only it wasn't. No sooner had they entered the dining hall than a girl from the cabin next door to them came over. "We saw what happened last night!"

Luckily, Carolyn was out of earshot. Katie had spread Erin's message, so the cabin six girls just looked innocent. "What are you talking about?" Erin asked sweetly.

"We heard the noise and we looked out our window," the girl said. "What did those boys want, anyway?"

"Nothing," Katie said quickly. "They were just being silly. Listen, don't tell anyone else about it, okay?"

"Are you kidding? Everyone already knows!"

Erin's face fell. She should have known it was impossible to keep a secret at Sunnyside.

"Well, maybe Ms. Winkle won't hear about it," Katie said comfortingly to Erin as they got in line for their trays. But Erin was in agony. What if the older girls knew her sort-of boyfriend had led a panty raid on her cabin? She'd be humiliated!

She had just taken her tray and was heading toward the table when she found her way blocked. Andrea, one of the cabin nine girls, and another girl were standing there. "We heard about last night," Andrea said.

Erin clutched her tray tightly. "It was no big deal."

"That's not what we heard," the other girl said.

"Did your boyfriend really sneak across the lake to see you?" Andrea asked. "That's so romantic!"

Erin's mouth dropped open. She knew how rumors changed when they spread—but this was amazing!

"Really romantic," the other girl agreed. "He must be nuts about you to do something like that."

Erin recovered her wits and tried to sound nonchalant. "He's the impulsive type."

"We're dying to hear the whole story," Andrea said. "Why don't you come sit with us?"

Erin was stunned. The only other time she'd sat with the older girls was during color war—when age and cabin were less important than your team. "Um, okay!"

19

As they walked, she found out that the other girl's name was Georgina. They passed the cabin six table, and Erin avoided looking at her own cabin mates. She could imagine their expressions, though.

Maura Kingsley was at the table, along with two other girls. "Hi, Erin," Maura said. "You know Denise and Ilene."

"Hi." Erin sat down. She still couldn't believe she was here, at the very same table she'd been eyeing so longingly yesterday.

Maura was gazing at her thoughtfully. "I heard your boyfriend practically broke down your door last night."

"Well, not exactly." But the other girls were looking at her with such avid interest that she had to expand. And maybe exaggerate—just a little.

"He just does nutty things like that. He's a pretty wild and crazy guy."

"You mean, he's done that before?" Denise asked.

Erin hesitated. She decided she'd better not get in too deep. "No . . . but we haven't seen each other in weeks, so I guess he was feeling crazier than usual." She sighed wistfully. "It's felt like months."

"Oh, I know what you mean," Ilene said sym-

20

pathetically. "I've got this boyfriend back home, and I feel like I haven't seen him in years."

"Did he want you to sneak out?" Georgina asked.

"Oh sure," Erin said. "He was practically on his knees, begging. But I didn't."

"Good for you," Maura said with approval. "You have to keep guys in their place. Playing hard to get only makes them want you more."

"That's what I think too," Erin said. "I didn't want him to think he could just snap his fingers and I'd come running."

"He must be absolutely positively nuts about you," Ilene sighed.

Erin laughed lightly. "Well, I think it's just a crush. But you never know."

"At least you'll get to see him at the Eagle camp fire tomorrow night," Andrea remarked.

"Yeah, and we're thinking about asking Ms. Winkle to ask the Eagle director if we could have a special dancing area just for older campers," Maura told her.

Erin nodded enthusiastically, but she wondered if "older campers" would include her. Just then, a tall, gangly girl with short brown hair sat down at the table. When she smiled at Erin, she revealed a mouthful of silver. "Hi. I'm Phyllis."

21

She certainly didn't look like a typical cabin nine girl, Erin thought as she replied, "I'm Erin." She noticed that the other girls barely glanced at Phyllis.

"I like your hair," Denise said to Erin. "Is it streaked?"

"Highlighted. I'm thinking of cutting it."

The girls considered her hair thoughtfully. "It could be cute," Andrea said. "Short hair's very hot right now."

"You'd look like you had higher cheekbones," Ilene noted.

Denise had a suggestion. "Try wearing it up for a while and see how you like it before you cut it. Maybe you could do a French braid."

Erin lowered her head in shame. "I don't know how to do those."

"I'll braid it for you this afternoon," Georgina offered.

"Gee, thanks," Erin said gratefully.

"Girls, can I have your attention?" Everyone looked toward the front of the room where Ms. Winkle was standing. The camp director didn't look very happy.

"I'm afraid I have some disappointing news for you. It seems that some boys from Camp Eagle committed a major infraction of the rules.

Because of this, their camp fire tomorrow night has been canceled."

Groans echoed through the room. "Bobby must have gotten caught," Erin moaned. "Oh, I'm just going to kill him for this."

The other girls looked dismayed but sympathetic too. "Don't be too hard on him," Andrea advised. "After all, he did it for love."

The conversation turned to boys in general. Erin noticed that the other campers in the room were starting to leave. It was time to get back to the cabin for cleanup and inspection. But the girls at her table didn't seem inclined to leave.

"Um, don't you guys have to get back?" Erin asked.

"Oh, our counselor's pretty cool about cleanup," Maura said. "We hardly even make our beds."

Erin nodded, but she couldn't help glancing at the cabin six table. All the girls had gone. And Carolyn was definitely *not* cool about cleanup. "I guess I'd better go," she said reluctantly.

"See you at the pool," Denise called.

"Right," Erin said happily. It was free swim day—and they were expecting her to hang out with them! She felt as if she could fly all the way back to cabin six.

When she went into the cabin, everyone was busy straightening up. But Katie paused to give her a long, hard look. "Why were you sitting with *them?*"

Erin went to her bed and started smoothing her sheets. "Because they asked me to."

Megan gazed at her in dismay. "How can you sit at the same table with Maura Kingsley?"

"Oh, she's not so bad once you get to know her," Erin said. "And the other girls were really nice."

Trina wrinkled her nose. "I don't think that Andrea's so nice. She was awfully mean during color war. Remember how she and Maura lied to us about the knots in our sailboat rigging? They said Katie had done it, just to turn us against her. And they had tied those knots themselves!"

Katie chimed in. "And don't forget how Maura poured water all over my skit scenery and ruined it."

"That was just because of color war," Erin argued. "People get like that when they're competing."

Sarah raised her eyebrows over the rim of her glasses. "If you ask me, Maura doesn't need a war to be mean. She's just that way naturally."

"I didn't ask you," Erin snapped. Then she

24

sighed. "Listen, just because I had breakfast with them doesn't make them my best friends."

"I should hope not," Katie stated. "You're still a cabin six girl, Erin. And don't forget it!"

Erin nodded in resignation. She knew Katie wouldn't let her forget it. "But that doesn't mean I can't have other friends too."

An uncomfortable silence filled the room. Finally, Trina changed the subject. "What time's the volleyball game today?"

"Three o'clock," Katie said. "And we're all playing, so don't be late, okay? We'll meet in front of the activities hall."

Erin just managed to finish making her bed when Carolyn came in for inspection. As soon as that was over, the girls began changing into their bathing suits.

Erin went over to the mirror and lifted her hair off her shoulders. A French braid would look really chic, she decided.

"Are you still thinking about cutting your hair?" Sarah asked.

"Andrea thinks it would make my cheekbones look higher."

Megan gazed at her in puzzlement. "Why would you want your cheekbones to look higher?"

Erin was on the verge of explaining that all

25

the top models had high cheekbones. But then she realized Megan couldn't possibly understand. None of them could.

"Never mind."

Chapter 3

"Hey, Erin!"

Coming through the gate around the swimming pool, Erin turned in the direction of the voice. Georgina was waving to her. She was sitting on the edge of the pool at the shallow end with Andrea and Denise. Erin waved back.

A girl from cabin five ran up to them. "You guys want to have a relay race?"

"Sure," Katie said. The others agreed and followed Katie to the deep end. Erin lingered at the gate.

"Erin, c'mon!" Katie called over her shoulder. But Erin still hesitated. When Georgina waved to her—had she been inviting Erin to join them?

"Erin, let's go!" Katie yelled. The girls had formed two lines for their relay, and they were waiting for her.

Erin started toward them, but she tossed one

more quick glance at Georgina and the others. Georgina waved again, and this time Erin was sure. She *was* beckoning Erin.

"You guys go ahead," she called to her cabin mates. And without waiting for a response, she hurried over to the shallow end.

She'd observed in the past how the cabin nine girls never went in the water on free swim days when there were no lessons. They always sat in that same spot, dangling their feet in the water. Or they lay on towels, sunbathing.

When she got closer, she saw Maura and Ilene lying facedown behind the others. Sitting down on the edge next to Georgina, she didn't dare look back at her cabin mates in the relay line. She had a feeling they were all staring at her.

"I've got some good news for you," Georgina said. "Your boyfriend wasn't sent home."

"How do you know?" Erin asked.

"I just saw Ms. Winkle. She said they just got tons of demerits and they're on probation."

Andrea's face was sympathetic. "I guess that means you won't be seeing him for a while."

Erin sighed. "And we don't even get to have that camp fire with them."

Maura joined them at the edge of the pool. "Good grief. What are those kids doing?"

Erin looked. Sarah was swimming past, just

28

behind a girl from cabin five. They were stroking furiously. At the other end of the pool, they could hear other girls screaming and cheering them on.

"They're having a relay race," Erin explained.

"That's idiotic," Maura stated. "The best thing about free swim days is that you don't have to go into the water."

Andrea nodded. "And we don't have to dash back to the cabin to wash and dry our hair. It's such a pain. There's only one electric outlet so we have to take turns. It takes ages."

"I know," Erin agreed fervently. "It's a pain. Then I'm always late for the next activity." Actually, she didn't have it as bad as they did, though. She was the only one in her cabin who insisted on blow-drying her hair. "At least I don't have to wait to use the outlet. The other girls in my cabin are perfectly willing to go out with wet heads. Can you believe that?"

"That's weird," Georgina said. "I'd never let anyone see me like that." She touched her perfectly layered cut. "Besides, if I let it dry in the sun, it wouldn't look right."

Erin thought about how her own cabin mates laughed when she took her time carefully drying her hair. These girls would never do that.

Another pair of relay swimmers passed them, closer to the edge. "They're splashing me," Maura complained. "And look at the others, screaming like this is the Olympics or something. Honestly, Erin, how can you stand sharing a cabin with them?"

Erin shrugged. "I've always been in that cabin."

"But they seem so much younger than you," Denise commented.

Erin preened. "I guess I matured faster than they did."

"That's too bad for you," Andrea said. "We've all been together for years too. But we all matured at the same time."

"Except for Phyllis," Maura added with a sneer. "Look at her."

Erin squinted. She could see Phyllis on the other side, swimming laps. Actually, she looked pretty good with her even strokes and neat kicks.

"She's getting muscles in her arms," Andrea noted. "That's so gross."

"She really is getting pretty nerdy," Georgina said. She giggled. "We spend a lot of time avoiding her. She can't even talk about anything normal."

Denise shook her head ruefully. "Would you

believe she brought a chess set to camp? And she honestly expected us to let her teach us how to play."

"Don't forget about her stamp collection," Andrea added. "She trades with the kids in cabin four!"

Erin rolled her eyes. Cabin four girls were nine years old! What could a thirteen-year old possibly have in common with them?

"I wish we could arrange a trade," Georgina said. "Erin for Phyllis."

"I don't think Ms. Winkle would ever allow that," Erin said.

"You're probably right," Maura said. "But it must be awful for you. Especially with Katie. I can't stand that girl."

Suddenly, Erin felt a little uncomfortable. "Oh, Katie's not that bad. A little bossy, but—"

"Bossy!" Maura snorted. "She's a total pain. The way she acted during color war drove me crazy."

"Well, it *was* a competition," Erin said uneasily. "You can't take things like that personally." Maura looked at her strangely, and Erin began to feel even more uncomfortable. Was she defending her cabin mates too much? She tried to think of a way to change the subject. "Isn't Darrell gorgeous?"

31

Everyone turned to look at the swimming coach, who was helping a camper get into a proper diving stance.

"No kidding," Georgina said. "I practically faint every time he speaks to me."

Erin nodded enthusiastically. "Whenever someone mentions his name, we always—" She stopped in the middle of her sentence. She had been about to show them the way all the cabin six girls put their hands over their hearts and pretended to swoon when they heard Darrell's name. But they might think that was pretty juvenile.

"You always what?" Georgina asked.

"Nothing. Listen, did you mean that about French braiding my hair today?"

"Sure! Come on over to cabin nine during free period at three o'clock. We'll do it then."

Three o'clock. That rang a bell in Erin's head. Was there something she was supposed to do at three? Well, it couldn't be that important.

"What do you have next?" Erin asked.

"Arts and crafts," Georgina said. "It's boring, but at least you don't sweat."

"Speaking of sweating," Andrea said, "we've got tennis this afternoon."

32

"Yuck," Georgina muttered. "Let's get out of it. It's too hot to run around today."

"Can you do that?" Erin asked in wonderment. "Get out of scheduled activities?"

"Sure," Andrea said. "Joan lets us get away with anything."

"I wish my counselor was like that," Erin said enviously. "She watches us like a hawk."

Just then Phyllis swam over to them and hoisted herself up.

"You splashed me!" Maura yelped.

"Sorry," Phyllis said, though she didn't look terribly regretful. Erin figured she must be used to Maura's attitude. "Why don't you guys come in? It's so hot!"

"No thanks," Andrea said coldly. Phyllis turned and swam off.

"What a dork," Maura grumbled.

Denise turned to Erin. "You know, she's never had a boyfriend."

"And her mother cuts her hair," Andrea put in.

Erin's eyebrows shot up. Poor Phyllis obviously didn't belong in cabin nine.

"Hey, Erin." Megan, with wet red curls hanging into her eyes, stood by her side. "C'mon, we have to go get ready for archery."

Erin was about to get up when Georgina

stopped her. "Skip archery. Come with us to arts and crafts."

"Yeah," Denise said. "Donna won't even notice."

She was probably right, Erin thought. There were always so many kids running around the arts and crafts cabin that the counselor wouldn't care if there was one more.

"Okay," she said.

Megan had been listening to this conversation with wide eyes. Erin couldn't blame her. Normally, every camper kept to her cabin's schedule.

But finally Megan nodded, and went back to the other cabin six girls. Erin watched her out of the corner of her eye. She could see that Megan was reporting the conversation to the others.

A second later, Katie appeared by her side. "Erin, we're supposed to be going to archery."

Maura gave her a mocking look. "Do you always do what you're supposed to do?"

Andrea giggled. "Afraid your counselor might scold you?"

Erin squirmed. She didn't really like the way they were talking to Katie. And she felt like she should say something in her cabin mate's defense. But at the same time, she didn't want to jeopardize her position.

"It's just this once, Katie. Archery's no big deal."

Georgina stretched and turned her head to the sky. "This sun feels great. Hey guys, let's not even go to arts and crafts. Let's stay here and work on our tans."

Katie's face was serious. "Too much sun is bad for your skin. You could end up with wrinkles. Or worse."

The cabin nine girls started laughing. Even Erin had to admit Katie sounded awfully prissy. Katie glared at them, and then directed herself to Erin. "Look, do what you want. We'll cover for you if the counselor notices you're missing. See you later."

"Okay," Erin called after her. "Thanks!"

But she didn't see Katie later, except from a distance. She ended up spending the entire day with the cabin nine girls. She sat with them at lunch and realized that their counselor, Joan, never sat with them. That meant they were free to talk about anything.

Maura was looking at Phyllis. "You know, Phyllis, you should start tweezing your eyebrows."

"Why?" Phyllis asked.

35

"Because they're too hairy."

Phyllis grinned. "Too hairy for what?"

"Guys don't like bushy eyebrows," Andrea said in a severe voice.

Phyllis made a who-cares gesture. Then she pulled out a book and propped it in front of her lunch. The others exchanged looks.

"Have you ever kissed Bobby?" Ilene asked Erin.

Erin bit her lip. "Oh sure," she lied. It actually wasn't a total lie. She'd intended to let him kiss her once. They'd sneaked away together from a camp fire Sunnyside had hosted. But they'd been caught by counselors before they could really do it.

"Is he a good kisser?" Denise wanted to know.

Erin made a nonchalant gesture. "So-so. Not as good as my boyfriend Alan back home." Another little white lie.

"My parents won't even let me date yet," Denise complained bitterly.

"Mine won't either," Erin hastened to assure her.

"I have to sneak out of the house just to see my boyfriend," Denise continued.

"Me too," Erin said. The lies were getting easier.

After lunch, she was summoned by Carolyn to go to arts and crafts. But she only stayed a few minutes before sneaking out and meeting the older girls for ice cream. Then it was free period, and they all went over to cabin nine.

Georgina sat Erin in a chair and went to work on her hair, while the others sprawled on their beds. "Camp is getting so boring," Maura complained. "There hasn't been anything exciting happening since color war."

"I know," Andrea said. "I was really looking forward to that camp fire at Eagle tomorrow night. Who knows when they'll invite us again."

"You know what we need?" Denise sat up. "We need to come up with something really wild and different to do."

"Like what?" Ilene asked.

"I don't know," Denise admitted. "Anybody got any brilliant ideas?"

Erin wondered if they were thinking about pranks, like the kind Katie always wanted to pull on other cabins. She suspected they had something different in mind. She didn't have any ideas anyway. It took all her concentration to keep from wincing while Georgina pulled at her hair.

Suddenly Maura jumped up. "I've got it!"

Everyone looked at her expectantly. Maura started pacing the room. "This would be really wild!"

"Tell us," Andrea demanded.

Maura faced them triumphantly. "Let's do what Erin's boyfriend did!"

Erin looked at her in bewilderment. "Throw pebbles at someone's cabin window at night?"

Maura nodded. "But not here. We'll sneak over to Camp Eagle!"

Erin gasped. "Are you serious?"

"Yeah! We'll sneak out late, get canoes, and row them across the lake."

"That's a fabulous idea," Andrea shrieked. "Can't you just picture their faces!"

"I love it!" Denise crowed. "Let's do it tonight!"

Erin could feel her heart thumping rapidly. "Tonight?"

"Sure! Why not?"

Erin could think of a million reasons. It was scary. It was dangerous. Canoeing in the dark— they could tip over and drown! Besides . . .

"What if we get caught?" she asked weakly. "We'd be in major trouble."

"We won't get caught if we're careful," Georgina replied.

Maura was eyeing Erin suspiciously. "What's the matter? Don't you have any guts?"

"Of course I do," Erin said, trying to sound positive. "I—I think it's a great idea."

"We'll meet at eleven-thirty," Maura decided, "down by the lake where the canoes are docked. Okay?"

Erin swallowed. She pictured the dark lake and the long ride across it. Then she took a deep breath. "Okay."

"And Bobby can see your new look!" Georgina announced. "Check it out, guys. Isn't this great?"

The others oohed and ahhed over Erin's French braid. Erin went to look in the mirror. She gasped in pleasure. It was amazing how a simple hairstyle could make her look so much more sophisticated.

"Gee, thanks, Georgina." Then she checked her watch. "Wow, it's just about rest period. I better get back." She smiled apologetically. "Carolyn always checks on us."

Maura made a face. "It sounds like you have a baby-sitter instead of a counselor."

She was right, and Erin felt embarrassed. "Well, I don't want her to start watching me too carefully. Especially if we're sneaking out tonight."

"Good point," Georgina said. "You go back and be a good girl. And we'll see you at the lake tonight."

Erin raced back to cabin six. By the time she ran in the door, she was out of breath. "Hi," she said to the others. "What do you think of my hair?"

She plopped down on her bed. And suddenly she realized that they were all staring at her with grim expressions.

She touched her braid. "What's the matter? Don't you like it?"

"Where were you?" Katie burst out. "We had a volleyball game! And we had to forfeit because you didn't show up!"

She'd forgotten all about it. And she was just about to apologize profusely when she caught herself. Volleyball game. Big deal. Kids' stuff. They all might as well realize that she wasn't into that kind of thing anymore.

"Sorry," she said coolly. She picked up a magazine and started leafing through it.

"Is that all you can say?" Katie asked. "How could you forget this game?"

Erin lifted her eyes from the magazine and gazed at Katie steadily. Then, very casually, she shrugged.

"I've got more important things on my mind."

40

Carolyn opened her door. "Girls, it's rest period. I don't want to hear any talking in here."

For once, Erin was happy to oblige. After all, she had a pretty big secret. And if they couldn't talk, at least she wouldn't run the risk of letting it slip.

Chapter 4

Erin was getting nervous. It was ten-thirty, and no one seemed even close to going to bed. True, they were all dressed for bed, in shortie pajamas or tee shirts. But Sarah was reading. Megan, Trina, and Katie were playing Monopoly. And no one looked the least bit sleepy.

Erin watched as Trina threw the dice. "Six," Katie announced.

"Katie, I can count," Trina said. She moved her little thimble, and then reached for a card. Katie leaned over to see it.

"Go to jail!" she screeched. " 'Go directly to jail. Do not pass go. Do not collect two hundred dollars.' "

"Katie, I can read, too!" Trina put her thimble in the jail corner.

Erin knelt down next to them and examined the game. They all had plenty of money left.

This game could go on all night! Wearily, she pushed up the sleeves of her nightgown.

"Erin, why are you wearing that long gown?" Trina asked. "It's so warm tonight."

"I don't know. I guess I just felt like it." She couldn't very well tell them she was wearing this gown to conceal the fact that she was fully dressed underneath. She stretched out her arms and opened her mouth wide in an exaggerated yawn. "I'm exhausted."

Katie looked at her skeptically. "How come? It's not like you did anything very strenuous today. Like play volleyball."

"Look, I said I was sorry. I just forgot, that's all." She got up. "I'm going to sleep. I hope you guys aren't planning to keep the lights on much longer." She went back to her bed and lay down, resting her head carefully on the pillow so she wouldn't mess up her braid. Of course, she really wasn't going to sleep. But maybe the others would follow her example.

Lying there, her eyes wide open, she shivered even though the room was very warm. She thought about the adventure that lay ahead. She wasn't exactly looking forward to it. The idea of being out on that dark lake at night, doing something that was totally forbidden made her feel queasy.

And she couldn't even get excited at the prospect of seeing Bobby. He'd acted so goofy the last time she saw him. He'd probably behave even goofier tonight, maybe even embarrass her in front of the older girls.

But she couldn't back out. The others would think she was a goody-goody, a chicken, no fun at all.

She ought to be pleased she'd been invited to go along. After all, that meant they were accepting her as one of them. I'm going, she told herself sternly. I'll have a wild adventure, and it'll be great fun. And maybe if I keep telling myself that, I'll believe it.

But before the great adventure could begin, her cabin mates had to go to sleep. So she just lay there and waited.

She was just about ready to demand lights out when she heard some yawns. "Let's finish tomorrow," Trina said. And then there was a chorus of good nights. The lights went out, and this time, thank goodness, Sarah didn't pull out a flashlight to read under the covers.

Erin checked her watch. It was eleven-ten. She had to wait a little longer to make sure everyone was really sleeping. It seemed like hours went by, but when she looked at her watch again, only five minutes had passed. She waited a little longer, until all she heard was steady, even breathing. And she decided to take a chance.

Slowly and quietly, she got out of bed and slipped off her nightgown. It was too dark to see if her shorts and shirt were wrinkled, but there was nothing she could do if they were. Quickly, she stuffed a blanket and the pillow under her sheets and hoped anyone getting up in the middle of the night would think the mound under the sheet was her. She picked up the shoes she'd placed by her bed, and barefoot, tiptoed toward the door.

She almost made it. Her hand was actually on the knob when she heard a soft voice. "What are you doing?"

Reluctantly, she lifted her eyes. Katie was sitting up in bed, looking down at her.

Well, she couldn't exactly say "nothing." "Going out," she whispered.

She couldn't see Katie's face too clearly, but she could imagine her expression.

"Where?"

Beneath Katie, Trina stirred. Erin put a finger to her lips. Katie then climbed down from her bed. She grabbed Erin's hand and practically dragged her into the bathroom. Closing the

45

door, she confronted her. "Where are you going?"

"None of your business," Erin replied.

Katie folded her arms. "Tell me. If you don't, I'm waking Carolyn."

The two girls gazed steadily at each other. Erin knew she had no choice. "If I tell you, you have to promise you'll keep it a secret. You can't tell anyone. Okay?"

Katie nodded.

"I'm going across the lake to Eagle with some of the cabin nine girls."

Katie's mouth fell open. "Erin, that's stupid! And it's dangerous!"

Erin brushed her objection aside. "There will be six of us. It's not like I'm going alone. C'mon, Katie, I thought you'd understand. You're always breaking rules and doing crazy things."

"But this—this is different!"

"Why? Because I'm going out with girls you don't like?"

"It's just such a dumb thing to do!" Katie made a disgusted face. "Sneaking off to a boys' camp. It's a dumb rule to break!"

"You think it's dumb? Well, I think those silly pranks you like to pull are dumb. And childish!" She looked at her watch and gasped. It was almost eleven-thirty. "I've gotta go."

Katie was actually speechless, and Erin didn't wait for her to recover her voice. She hurried out, still on her toes, and left the cabin.

At least she knew Katie wouldn't tell. That was something she could count on. Cabin six girls had a pact. They never told on each other, no matter what anyone did.

Once outside, she pulled on her shoes. Then she ran through the silent camp and down to the lake.

The others were already there. "See! I told you she'd come," Georgina said to Maura.

"We're going three to a canoe," Maura informed Erin. "That way, we can trade off rowing. C'mon, let's go."

Within seconds, two canoes began drifting away from the bank of the lake. Erin was rowing in one, with Georgina rowing on the other side and Denise in the middle.

"This is so cool!" Denise exclaimed.

Erin wished she could agree, but her arms were already aching. That extra person in the canoe added a lot of weight.

She could see Georgina straining too, but she didn't look bothered by it. "It's beautiful out here!"

And Erin had to admit she was right. The quiet of the lake, the darkness, the stars—it wasn't scary at all. In fact, it was very peaceful. In unison, they paddled and talked quietly. They didn't need to whisper. No one could hear them out here. But somehow the atmosphere called for quiet voices.

"Do you know what cabin Bobby is in?" Denise asked Erin.

"No."

"We'll just pick the nearest cabin and throw pebbles at the window," Georgina said. "And whoever comes out can tell us what cabin your boyfriend is in."

"But what if we get a baby cabin? You know, nine year olds or something. They might make a fuss and their counselor will catch us."

Georgina pondered this. "Good point." Then she brightened. "We'll peek in through the windows first and try to see what age they are."

Erin marveled at her intelligence. Suddenly, Denise clapped her hands. "I see land!"

Sure enough, the lights on Camp Eagle's lakefront revealed that they were close. As they reached shallow water, they jumped out of the canoe and pulled it to shore. They met the girls from the other canoe on the bank of the lake, and put on the shoes they'd been carrying.

"Yuck, we should have brought a towel," Maura said. "My legs are wet."

"We'll have to remember to bring one next time," Andrea remarked. Erin wondered about this. Were they planning to make this a regular event?

"Has anyone been here before?" Ilene asked.

"I have," Georgina said. "My brother used to come here. The cabins are this way." She started toward the road, and the others followed.

It was the oddest feeling, walking through a strange camp in the middle of the night. Every now and then someone would start giggling nervously, but she was always hushed by the others. The mere thought of getting caught kept Erin silent. She had a pretty good suspicion what the consequences would be. Ms. Winkle wouldn't let them off with a few demerits and probation.

When they reached the first cabin, Maura pulled them together for a consultation. "Their windows are open," she whispered.

"But they're too high!" Erin said softly. "How are we going to look in?"

"I've got an idea," Georgina said. Swiftly she explained. Then she and Denise got down beneath the windows on their hands and knees. Ilene climbed on top of them, putting one foot on each back. And she peered in through the window.

Then she hopped down. "They look like they're at least thirteen."

"Now what do we do?" Andrea asked.

"We do what they did," Georgina said. "We throw pebbles at the window."

"But the windows are open," Erin protested.

Georgina's eyes twinkled. "So much the better. Maybe they'll land on their heads!"

Quickly the girls gathered up small pebbles. Then they separated, two at each window. Softly, Georgina said, "One, two, three—throw!"

They tossed their pebbles into the window. And then they waited with bated breath.

A minute later, a sleepy-looking boy appeared at the window. Erin squinted. He looked vaguely familiar.

He stared in astonishment at them. "What are you doing here?"

Georgina nudged Erin. She cleared her throat nervously. "Uh, do you know what cabin Bobby Crawford is in?"

The boy grinned. "Yeah, he's in here."

And then Erin realized why he looked familiar. He was one of the boys who'd come with Bobby to Sunnyside! The boy disappeared from the window. A few seconds later, he reappeared—with Bobby.

He looked stunned too. "Erin! What's going on?"

Aware that the other girls were watching her, Erin smiled coyly. "Just returning your visit. You came to see me, so I've come to see you. And I brought some friends."

She wasn't sure how she'd expected Bobby to react. Thrilled? Flattered? She certainly hadn't anticipated the expression she saw clearly on his face: horror.

"Listen, I'm already in enough trouble! You girls better get out of here." He closed the window and disappeared from view.

Erin wanted to crawl in a hole. She wished the earth would open up and swallow her. "It doesn't look like your boyfriend's too happy to see you," Maura said in a snotty voice.

Erin didn't know what to say. Luckily, Georgina took over. "I think he's noble. He's probably being watched very carefully, and he doesn't want Erin to get into any trouble."

"What do we do now?" Andrea asked.

"Let's try another cabin," Georgina said, but then she stopped. "Do you guys hear something?"

Erin did. And the sound was unmistakable. It

was a car. It was coming their way. And now she could see the headlights.

"Hide behind the cabin!" Maura yelled. Everyone ran. For one split second, Erin froze. Then she took off too, behind the others.

But she tripped. Suddenly, she found herself facedown on the ground. The shock of the fall paralyzed her. Frantically, she tried to pull herself up. But it was too late.

"Hey! What are you doing?"

It was her worst nightmare come true. She heard the car door open and someone coming toward her. Cold tremors engulfed her as she got up and faced her accuser.

"Teddy!"

She couldn't believe her eyes. It was the handyman from Sunnyside, the guy her counselor used to go with.

Teddy looked just as amazed as she was. "Erin! What—what are you doing here?"

Erin thought frantically. She was aware that the other girls were just behind the cabin, listening to every word. "I, I couldn't sleep," she said lamely. "I decided to take a walk."

Teddy's expression was dubious. "Across the lake?"

Erin was fully aware of the fact that going

around the lake on the road was at least ten miles. "No . . ."

"How did you get here?" Teddy asked.

Erin wished she had Megan's imagination. But she did the best she could. "I, uh, walked down to our side of the lake. And there was this guy there, from Eagle. He came over in a canoe. He wanted me to come back here with him. So I did."

"Why?"

"I don't know. Just for an adventure."

"Where's this boy now? Who is he?"

"I don't know."

She could tell he didn't believe her story. He put his hands on his hips and spoke sternly. "Okay, where are the others?"

Erin gazed at him innocently. "What others?"

"The rest of you cabin six girls. Carolyn isn't going to be very happy when she hears about this."

Erin shook her head. "I'm all by myself."

Now Teddy looked angry. "You came over here by yourself, with some boy you didn't even know?"

Erin nodded. Teddy took her arm and led her to the car. "Get in," he ordered. Meekly, she obeyed.

Teddy started the engine and they drove off. "What you did tonight, Erin, wasn't just a silly prank. It was stupid and dangerous. Do you realize that?"

He sounded like Katie. But Erin responded as humbly as she could. "I know. I'm sorry. Are you going to tell on me?"

"Don't you think I should?"

"Oh, Teddy, please don't tell! I'll be in so much trouble. Ms. Winkle will call my parents and send me home! I'll be grounded for the rest of my life! I'm sorry I did this, I'm really truly sorry. Please don't tell on me!"

She looked at him sideways to see if this was having any effect. He was looking straight ahead at the road, and she couldn't tell. So she did the only thing she could think of. She burst into tears.

It worked. "All right, all right. I won't tell. But if you ever try something like this again, I *will* report you. Do you understand?"

"Yes."

"And do you honestly promise me you'll never cross that lake again without permission?"

Erin gulped. Could she do that? What if the girls wanted to do this again? Even though she wasn't a goody-goody, there was something about making a promise when you knew you might break it that made her feel—bad.

But there was no other way.

"Okay. I promise."

Chapter 5

Erin avoided Katie's eyes the next morning as they dressed for breakfast. But she could feel those eyes, curious and suspicious. She knew Katie was dying to hear what happened last night. But there was no way she was going to talk about it in front of the others. Even though they wouldn't tell on her, she didn't want to take the chance of rumors spreading. Besides, she hadn't decided exactly what she was going to tell Katie anyway.

But Katie wasn't about to let too much time go by before hearing the story. As the group left the cabin, she pulled Erin back. As usual, she didn't beat around the bush.

"Okay, what happened? Did you go over to Eagle?"

"Oh, sure," Erin said casually. "It was no big deal, really."

Katie's eyes grew larger. "What did you do when you got there?"

"We found Bobby's cabin. And then . . ." She paused, still trying to think up a good story.

"And then what?" Katie pressed.

"The guys came outside. Of course, Bobby was *thrilled.* We just hung around and talked. And then we came back."

"That's all?" Katie looked disappointed.

"Well, what did you expect?" Erin asked. "Did you think we were going to roll the cabin in toilet paper?" That seemed like the kind of thing Katie would do.

"But what's the point of going to all that trouble if you're just going to hang out?"

Erin gave Katie her best patronizing look. "Katie, when you grow up, you'll understand. Maybe."

"I still think it was a dumb risk to take. You're not going to do it again, are you?"

Erin fervently hoped not. But all she did was smile mysteriously. Then she ran on ahead to the dining hall.

She spotted the cabin nine girls, already seated at their table. As soon as she collected her tray, she started toward them. But when she passed the cabin six table, Megan called out to her. "Erin! Aren't you going to sit with us anymore?"

Erin paused. Megan's innocent face looked sort of sad. It gave her a funny feeling. And the others were looking at her too, with curious and concerned expressions. She didn't know what to say.

Luckily, Carolyn spoke up. "There's no rule that says each cabin has to sit together. It's not so terrible to want to get to know some of the other campers."

Erin smiled at her gratefully. Carolyn was really okay, even if she did watch them all a lot more than cabin nine's counselor did.

Trying to ignore the fact that her cabin mates were still giving her those peculiar looks, she walked on to the cabin nine table. And it was worth leaving her old friends behind for the welcome she got from her new ones.

"Erin! You're here!" Georgina exclaimed.

"We thought for sure you'd be on your way home," Ilene said. She glanced down at the end of the table, where Phyllis sat apart with her book propped in front of her. Then she lowered her voice. "What happened?"

Erin sat down. "I begged and pleaded and Teddy finally said he wouldn't turn me in."

"And you told him you were all alone." Denise beamed at her. "We heard you! That was really great of you."

Even Maura acknowledged that. "Yeah, you saved our skins."

Erin basked in the praise. "It was nothing," she said modestly. "It was my own fault for tripping. And I'd never tell on you guys." She got a warm feeling from the satisfied smiles that greeted her statement.

"We should make you an honorary cabin nine camper," Georgina said. Just then, Phyllis got up.

"I'm going to get seconds. Anyone want anything?"

The others shook their heads, and Phyllis went off. "I wish we could make you a real cabin nine camper," Ilene said. "If only we could get rid of Phyllis."

"Well, we have to think of some way to get rid of her tonight," Andrea said. She turned to Erin. "My mother sent this huge box of goodies, and we're having a feast."

"You're invited," Georgina added.

"Thanks!" Erin replied.

"And Andrea came up with another great scheme," Georgina said. "Tell her, Andrea."

"We're going to sneak away from camp for a full day," Andrea announced, "and go to Pine

Ridge. We'll go shopping and hang out at the pizza parlor."

"For the whole day?" Erin shifted uneasily in her seat. It was one thing to get her cabin mates to cover for her when she missed an activity or two. But would she be able to get away for a full day? And then another thought occurred to her. "How will we get there?"

"Hitchhike," Andrea said. "We'll walk up to the main road and thumb our way into town."

Now Erin felt really nervous. She knew how dangerous hitchhiking could be. But if she mentioned this, they might think she was a coward. Well, she'd deal with it when it happened.

"There goes Ms. Winkle," Denise noted. Erin turned and saw the camp director heading to the front of the room for her usual morning announcements. For a moment, she was nervous. What if Teddy had told on her after all? But Ms. Winkle didn't seem particularly distressed.

"Girls, I know how disappointed you are about the Eagle camp fire being canceled. So, tomorrow night we're going to have our own."

"Will the Eagle boys be coming?" a camper called out.

"No," Ms. Winkle said. "I'm afraid their privileges have been canceled for a week, due to those silly boys who broke curfew." She shook her head regretfully. "I'm certainly glad that none of you girls would ever think of doing anything like that."

The girls at Erin's table exchanged grins and muffled giggles. "If only she knew," Georgina murmured, her eyes twinkling.

"What happened last night after I left?" Erin asked them.

"We went to the cabin next door," Maura said, "and *those* boys were a lot cooler, and older too. They're fourteen. They came outside and we walked all around the camp with them."

"We're going back there Friday night to meet them," Andrea told her. "And I'll bet you'll meet someone a lot more interesting than Bobby."

Erin nodded, smiling. But somehow she couldn't feel wildly enthusiastic about another adventure like that especially after her promise to Teddy. And hanging out with boys who were fourteen . . . she'd never admit it, but the idea was just a little terrifying.

She noticed that the cabin six girls were leaving their table. "I better get back to my cabin," she said. "I'll see you guys at the pool."

She hurried out and caught up with the others on their way back to the cabin. "Gee, you're actually going to walk with us?" Katie asked. "How nice of you."

Erin ignored the sarcasm. "What are we doing in swimming today?"

"Diving," Trina told her.

"Yuck," Erin commented.

"I thought you liked diving," Megan said. "And you're good at it."

"Yeah, but it'll ruin my braid," Erin replied.

"Oh, that's too bad," Katie remarked. "And your mascara will run, too." Once again, her voice dripped with sarcasm.

Erin gritted her teeth. Katie was being so obnoxious.

"Diving," Sarah murmured. "I still don't feel like I've got the hang of it. I keep forgetting the position."

"Maybe Erin could help you," Trina suggested.

Sarah looked at Erin hopefully. "Will you?"

"Sure," Erin said, but her thoughts were somewhere else. Even as they entered the cabin and started making beds, she went through the routine automatically, barely aware of what she was doing. She had other things to think about.

Hitchhiking to Pine Ridge. Another midnight trip to Eagle. Obviously, these were adventures the cabin nine girls enjoyed. Then why couldn't she get more excited about their ideas? Okay, maybe they were a little older than she, but they were acting like she was one of them. She should be mature enough to handle the same kind of experiences they liked. She'd just have to be more gutsy if she was going to keep up with them.

Later, when they headed out for the pool, Erin found herself walking next to Carolyn. "Thanks for sticking up for me this morning," she told her counselor. She lowered her voice. "Sometimes these guys can be so childish."

Carolyn smiled. "But they *are* your friends, Erin. Don't forget that. Of course, that doesn't mean you can't have other friends too. But don't leave your old friends behind."

Erin kicked at a pebble. "But they wouldn't fit in with my new friends. They—they're not sophisticated enough."

"Oh, I'm not saying you all have to hang around together all the time. Just remember that your cabin mates really care about you."

Erin wasn't so sure of that. "If they really cared about me, they wouldn't hassle me about making new friends."

Carolyn seemed to be choosing her words carefully. "Maybe they're just afraid you're getting in over your head." Erin gazed at her in puzzlement. What was that supposed to mean?

The scene at the pool was much more organized than it had been the day before. They were supposed to be demonstrating their diving ability, and Darrell was pairing the girls to practice.

"I'm giving you ten minutes to work together. Then I want to see what each of you can do."

Erin was paired with Sarah, and she knew Darrell had a reason for this. Sarah had only just learned to swim that summer, and she was still a little awkward.

Plus, she was very nervous about diving in front of the others. Even though they'd all been working on their diving for several weeks, she didn't have much confidence. "Let me see you do one," she said to Erin.

Erin patted her French braid a fond farewell. "Okay." She stood on the ledge, and dived off. When she got out of the water, Sarah's face was envious. "You barely made a ripple in the water. I'll never be able to do it like that."

"Sure you can. The secret is that you just have to get into the right position before you push off. Like this." She demonstrated the proper stance. Sarah did a poor imitation.

"No, no, arch your back. And keep—"

"Hey, Erin!"

She looked up. On the other side of the pool, Georgina was motioning to her. Sarah saw this too.

"Aren't you going to help me?" she asked plaintively.

"I'll be right back," Erin promised. She went around the pool.

"Maura just had a fantastic idea," Georgina told her.

What now? Erin wondered. She looked at Maura apprehensively.

Maura was looking very pleased with herself. "You know how we want to get rid of Phyllis tonight? Well, I came up with a way to do it."

"How?" Erin asked.

"We're going to tell her Ms. Winkle wants to see her right away."

Erin's forehead puckered. "But when she gets there, Ms. Winkle will just send her back."

Maura smiled smugly. "Ms. Winkle won't even be there. I heard her talking about going to visit a friend in Pine Ridge this evening. Phyllis will be sitting there waiting for her all night."

"Oh." Erin had to admit it was a pretty clever idea. Sort of mean, though. And Phyllis would eventually find out they'd tricked her. She'd probably feel awful.

But on the other hand, Phyllis was a nerd, and this was the way nerds got treated. Besides, who was Erin to question them?

"Come on over around eight," Georgina told her.

Just then Darrell blew his whistle. "Okay, I want to see some great diving! Take your places."

"Yeah, I'll see you at eight," Erin said, and walked quickly back to the other side where the cabin six girls were lined up. As she passed Sarah, there was no way she could miss her woebegone face. With a sinking feeling, she realized she hadn't finished showing Sarah the proper position. Well, it was too late to do anything about that now. Sarah would just have to watch the others and copy them.

Even so, she felt a little pang when Sarah turned slightly and gave her a reproachful look. Darrell started at one end of the line of girls and blew a short blast on his whistle. The first girl dived in. She was a little wobbly but not terrible. He blew again, and the next girl hit the water. On down the line he went. Out of the corner of her eye, Erin could see the fear growing on Sarah's face.

And when it was Sarah's turn, she goofed. She didn't tuck her chin in or bend her knees. And her dive turned into a belly flop.

Some of the campers, like Maura and Andrea, burst out laughing. When Sarah emerged from the water, they were still jeering. There was no way Sarah couldn't hear them.

But it's not my fault, Erin told herself. Sarah should have paid more attention last week when Darrell was demonstrating the techniques.

But she knew Sarah had a problem remembering things like that. And if Erin had just spent a few more minutes with her . . .

She pushed the thought from her mind and focused on getting ready for her own dive. But her concentration was off. And as she hit the water, she knew she hadn't been as good as usual.

The rest of the pool time was taken up with Darrell pointing out their faults and spending a few minutes individually with each of them. As soon as the session was over, Erin steeled herself to face Sarah.

Sarah had her head down, as if she was ashamed of showing her face. Erin felt a wave of pity. "Look, if you want, we can work on diving during free period today."

Sarah raised her head, and Erin was startled

to see the hostility in that usually sweet face. "Forget it. I wouldn't want to take you away from your *friends.*"

Erin was taken aback by her tone. When she recovered, she gave Sarah an equally cold look. "Suit yourself." And with her head high, she marched past Sarah without another glance.

Chapter 6

Erin got back to the cabin first, and she was glad to be alone. Right this moment, Sarah was probably telling the others how Erin hadn't helped her, and getting them all to blame Erin for her poor performance. Well, that's just too bad, she thought angrily.

She went into the shower. She took her time washing her hair, putting off the moment when she'd have to face them all. She knew how they'd treat her. They'd probably give her the silent treatment, like they did at the beginning of the summer when the boys from Camp Eagle were staying at Sunnyside while their own camp was being repaired. Katie had ordered them all to ignore the boys, and when she found out Erin was hanging out with Bobby, she got the others to stop speaking to Erin. They were such infants, Erin thought as she rubbed the conditioner furiously into her hair.

Finally, she had to get out. She wrapped herself in her bathrobe, took a deep breath, and went back into the cabin.

She'd expected to be greeted by a cold silence. To her surprise, they were all talking excitedly.

"What's going on?" she asked.

"We just found out that today's Carolyn's birthday!" Trina told her. "Laura, the counselor in cabin five, told us."

"And we're going to have a surprise party for her," Katie announced. "I'm going to see Ms. Winkle about getting a cake and other stuff. We're going to invite cabin five and some of the other counselors too, like Donna from arts and crafts."

Erin thought about how nice Carolyn had been to her lately. "That's a neat idea. When's the party?"

"Tonight at nine," Katie said. "We've got it all organized. Laura's going to come over around eight and tell Carolyn that Ms. Winkle wants to see her. Only Ms. Winkle won't even be there because she's going to Pine Ridge tonight."

Megan was hopping up and down. "So while Carolyn's sitting there and waiting for her, we'll decorate the cabin and set everything up."

"We're getting crepe paper streamers and balloons from arts and crafts," Sarah chimed in. In the excitement, she seemed to have forgotten her anger at Erin.

"Then Laura will go get Carolyn," Trina said. "When she gets here, we'll be hiding in the dark. And we'll all jump out and yell 'surprise'!"

Well, it wasn't the most original idea in the world, Erin thought, but Carolyn would love it. And then she remembered something.

"What's the matter?" Trina asked.

Erin realized her thoughts must be showing on her face. "Oh, nothing." Maybe it wouldn't be a problem. The cabin nine feast was at eight. The party was at nine. She'd just have to leave the feast a little early. It was no big deal. "Sounds great. I'll be here."

"You better be!" Katie was grinning as she said this. But Erin couldn't help thinking it sounded almost like a threat.

"Let it hang a little lower," Katie called across the room. She was standing on her top bunk, hooking one end of a crepe paper streamer over a beam. On the other side of the room, Trina was standing on Sarah's bed with the other end of the streamer.

In the middle of the room, there was a table with a big cake on it. Sarah and Megan were carefully placing candles between the flowers that decorated the top of the cake.

"It's too bad Carolyn has to sit in Ms. Winkle's office for an hour," Megan said. "I'll bet she's getting impatient already."

"She'll forget all about it when she sees this," Katie assured her. "Erin, where are you going?"

Erin stood at the door. "Um, I have to go see somebody."

Trina looked down at her anxiously. "Do you have your watch on? Remember, you have to be back before nine to surprise Carolyn."

"Sure, I know," Erin said quickly. She held up her hand to show Trina she had her watch on her wrist. "I'll see you guys in just a little bit."

It was already a few minutes after eight, and Erin walked rapidly toward cabin nine. She was halfway there when she saw Phyllis coming from that direction. And she remembered Maura's plan for getting rid of her.

Poor Phyllis. Well, at least she'd have Carolyn there to keep her company. But when the other counselor came to get Carolyn at nine, Phyllis would find out that Ms. Winkle wasn't even there. She'd know the other girls had set her up. She'd come back to the cabin hurt and angry that she hadn't been invited to the feast. But that probably wouldn't even bother the girls in cabin nine.

Suddenly, Erin was glad she was going to have to leave early. She really didn't want to witness Phyllis's return.

"Hi, Erin," Phyllis said as she approached.

"Hi," Erin said awkwardly. "Um, where are you headed?"

"To see some friends in cabin seven."

Erin tried not to look surprised. So the girls hadn't hit her with that lie about Ms. Winkle wanting to see her. Somehow that made her feel better.

But Phyllis's next words surprised her even more. "Are you going to my cabin for the feast?"

Erin's mouth dropped. She didn't know what to say. Phyllis smiled. "Don't worry, I know all about it. And I knew they wanted to get rid of me. So I told them I was going to see my friends. That way they wouldn't have to make up some story to get me out of the cabin."

Erin wondered how she could say that and still smile. "You—you don't get along with your cabin mates."

Phyllis's smile became wistful. "Not anymore. We used to, until this year. Then Maura and Andrea sort of took over, and now the others all follow anything they say and do."

"Why do you stay there? How can you stand it?"

"Because I keep hoping things will get better," Phyllis said simply. "See you later."

Erin tried to push the image of Phyllis's sad smile from her mind. She had a feast to go to—and it was already eight-fifteen.

"Here she is!" Georgina called out as Erin walked in. The cabin nine girls were sitting on the floor, with an incredible quantity of food surrounding them. Erin sat down, and Ilene passed her a plate of brownies.

"I just saw Phyllis," Erin said, taking a brownie. "I felt sort of sorry for her."

Andrea groaned. "Don't bother. She's so dorky."

"I wish we could think of a way to get rid of her permanently," Maura complained. "I keep waiting for some brilliant idea to hit me."

"She just doesn't fit in," Denise said. "Like you don't fit in at your cabin, Erin."

Erin nibbled at her brownie. "Mmm, these are good. I can't eat too much, though. We're having a party in cabin six for our counselor's birthday."

Andrea stared at her in disbelief. "You're having a party for your counselor? How dumb."

"It wasn't my idea," Erin said quickly. "It was Katie's."

"That figures," Maura commented. "She's just the type to kiss up to counselors."

"But Carolyn's not so bad," Erin began, and then stopped. They were all looking at her as if she was an alien.

"Erin, you told us yourself she watches you guys like a baby-sitter," Georgina reminded her.

Erin thought she'd better change the subject. "Are you still planning to hitchhike to Pine Ridge?"

Andrea nodded. "Yeah, next week. We figured we better go on free swim day. Darrell would notice if we weren't there for swimming lessons."

"You're going to go with us, aren't you?" Georgina asked.

Erin had a hard time swallowing the brownie in her mouth. "Uh, sure."

"And don't forget we're going back to Eagle Friday night," Denise reminded her. She hugged her knees to her chest and smiled dreamily. "Those guys were *so* cute."

"Hey, maybe we can all sneak into their pool and have a midnight swim," Georgina said.

"Everyone should wear their bathing suits under their shorts."

"Why bother?" Maura said lazily. "We could all go skinny-dipping."

This suggestion brought forth shrieks of laughter. Erin laughed along with them, but the mere idea sent shivers of horror through her.

"Hey, you want me to braid your hair again?" Georgina offered. "I need to do something with my hands so I won't eat so much."

Erin agreed, and Georgina got behind her. "We won't really go skinny-dipping," she whispered in Erin's ear. Erin smiled in relief. But even so, she still wasn't thrilled at the prospect of going there. After all, she had given Teddy her promise never to do it again.

She couldn't tell them that, though. They'd only laugh. "Is Teddy still hanging out with your counselor?" she asked them. Teddy used to go with Carolyn, but they'd broken up.

"No, Joan's out with this counselor from Eagle," Andrea said. This set them off on a discussion of who each counselor was seeing.

"Does Carolyn have a boyfriend now?" Denise asked Erin. Hearing Carolyn's name made Erin look at her watch. It was a quarter to nine.

"I don't think so. Listen, guys, I'm going to

have to take off. I'm supposed to be back before nine. It's a surprise party."

Maura made a face. "Surprise parties are so tacky."

"You can't leave now," Georgina said. "I'm right in the middle of your braid."

Well, she really didn't have to be there to yell surprise, Erin decided. No one would notice, as long as she didn't miss the whole party.

When they finished discussing the social life of each counselor, Maura introduced the subject of boyfriends in general. "Everyone has to tell about her first kiss. I'll go first." She then began a long story about a boy she met when her family went on a skiing holiday two years ago.

Andrea went next, talking about a school dance where she left her date and went off with a different guy. As they talked, Erin tried to think of an exciting story she could tell. She knew she wouldn't be able to top their stories, and she wasn't even sure she could match them. They'd all had so many more experiences than she'd had.

She liked hearing about them. Their stories made her think about possible experiences she might have, someday, when she was older. And she listened intently as each girl went into elaborate detail about everything from what she was wearing to what color the boy's eyes were. She was so caught up, she was barely aware that Georgina had finished her braid.

The stories went on and on, and became more interesting and more detailed with each girl. But it was getting closer to her turn, and she was nervous. She still hadn't thought of a way to make her one crummy little peck on the cheek from Alan back home sound more dramatic.

Then she glanced at her watch, and gasped. It was almost eleven! Had they really been talking for over two hours? She jumped up. "I've gotta go."

"But we haven't heard your story yet," Georgina objected.

"I'll tell it another time," Erin said hastily. "Look, I could get into real trouble for this!"

"Ooh, your baby-sitter might tell your mommy on you," Maura said in a nasty voice.

At least Georgina seemed understanding. "Erin's right, this isn't worth getting into trouble for." Her eyes twinkled. "Might as well save that for something big!"

"I'll see you later," Erin said. And she dashed out.

She ran all the way back to cabin six. As she approached, she could see the lights were still on, and she breathed more easily. She went in the door.

Katie and Trina were pulling down the streamers. Megan and Sarah were gathering paper plates and cups. But they all stopped suddenly when they saw Erin.

Erin managed a weak smile. "Where's the party?"

Katie's voice was icy. "You're too late. The party's over."

Chapter 7

From the expressions on their faces, Erin knew she'd be wasting her time offering apologies or excuses. They were too angry to listen. So, with her head high, she sauntered through the cabin, sat down on her bed, and picked up a magazine.

They weren't going to let her get away so easily, though. "Oh, Erin," Trina lamented. "How could you miss Carolyn's birthday party?"

Erin opened the magazine and pretended to be studying it intently. "I lost track of the time."

"Where were you?" Katie demanded.

Her tone got on Erin's nerves. Who did Katie think she was, anyway? She lifted her head and faced her. "I was at cabin nine."

Sarah tossed paper cups in the wastebasket with unusual force. "That figures. In other words, you were too busy having fun with your new friends to come to your own counselor's birthday party."

Erin forced herself to speak nonchalantly. "You're acting like it's such a big deal. What does it matter whether I was here or not?" She remembered what Maura had said. "Besides, surprise parties are tacky."

"Carolyn didn't think so," Trina said gently. "She was thrilled. And she wondered where you were."

Erin set her lips in a tight line. Her stomach was doing funny things. She must have eaten too many brownies. Or maybe it was something else. "Where's Carolyn now?"

"She walked the others back to cabin five," Trina said.

Megan twisted a lock of her hair. "Erin, how come you like those cabin nine girls better than us now?"

This was getting ridiculous. It was like a kindergarten conversation, when you fight with your best friend. Erin thrust the magazine aside and faced them. "I never said that. I just like hanging around with them. They're fun to be with, and they're interested in the same things I'm interested in."

"But they're not good for you," Katie said bluntly. "You think you're one of them, but you're not, really. They're too old for you. And they're getting you to do things you shouldn't be doing."

Erin shot her a warning look, but Katie didn't go into details. She just fixed stern eyes on Erin and looked like a teacher reprimanding her for cutting class. "Erin, if you keep hanging out with those girls, you're looking for trouble."

Erin gave her an equally fierce look. "Whatever I'm doing, it's none of your business."

The cabin door opened, and Carolyn walked in. Her face was flushed and excited. And when she spotted Erin, a relieved smile crossed her face. "Erin, I'm glad you're back. I was worried about you."

Erin couldn't meet her eyes. "Sorry I missed your party," she mumbled. She waited to hear Carolyn say something like, "that's okay," or "no problem," but she didn't. Her voice was soft when she said, "I'm sorry, too."

Thursday was a funny sort of day. Erin decided she'd better not skip out on any scheduled activities. Carolyn was annoyed enough with her already. And maybe if she spent an occasional day with her cabin mates, they wouldn't get so obnoxious when she spent time with the cabin nine girls.

So she went through the whole day with them, swimming, horseback riding, archery, arts and crafts. She even sat with them for all the meals. But she didn't say much to them—mainly because they weren't saying much to her.

It was very frustrating. Here she was, giving *them* her company instead of the people she really wanted to be with. And they didn't even appreciate it!

At least there was the camp fire that evening. She certainly wasn't going to spend it with them, singing dumb camp songs and throwing marshmallows at one another. As soon as they arrived, she left them and made her way through the groups of campers until she found the cabin nine girls.

"Where have you been all day?" Georgina asked.

Her question made Erin feel warm all over. These girls *wanted* her around.

She rolled her eyes in disgust. "The kids in my cabin were mad about my missing that dumb party last night. And Carolyn was kind of ticked off too. So I figured I'd better stick with them today. But they're acting like such jerks! You'd think I committed a major crime or something!"

Georgina was sympathetic. "Poor Erin. You just have to get out of that cabin."

"Yeah. But where would I go?"

Andrea and Maura exchanged looks. Then Andrea spoke. "Well, we just might have an empty space in our cabin pretty soon."

"You're kidding!" Erin exclaimed. "Is somebody leaving?"

"Maybe," Ilene said, shooting a furtive look at Maura.

They were all being very mysterious, but they looked pleased with themselves too. And it didn't take Erin long to figure out who must be leaving.

"Is Phyllis moving into another cabin?"

"No," Andrea said. "Guess again."

There was only one other possibility. "Is she going home?"

Maura smiled slyly. "She might be. If you'll help."

Erin's stomach started churning. What could they possibly want her to do to get Phyllis out of the cabin? Surely it couldn't be anything violent. "What do you mean?"

"Wait till you hear her idea," Denise chortled. "It's positively brilliant!"

Now Maura became very businesslike. "Do you know anything about computers?"

"A little," Erin admitted. "We use them at school. And my parents have one at home." She grinned. "I have a file on a disk that lists all the clothes I have. That way, I can make sure I don't wear the same thing twice in one week."

"Then you know how to put stuff on to a file and take stuff off," Maura said. Erin nodded, and Maura beamed at her.

"Excellent!" She scanned the area where they were sitting, as if to make sure no one could overhear them. Then she motioned to the other girls, and they gathered in closer.

"Ms. Winkle has a computer in her office," Maura told Erin. "I was in there one day and I saw her using it. She's got a file on each camper. She had to leave the office when I was there, so while she was out, I called up my file."

"What was on it?" Erin asked.

"The usual information. Parents' names, address, cabin number. Stuff like allergies or special diets, that sort of thing. And something else too." She paused dramatically.

"What?"

"Demerits. Everytime a camper gets a demerit, Ms. Winkle adds it to the file. She doesn't put in what the person got the demerit for, just the number."

Erin wondered how many demerits Maura

had, but she figured it wouldn't be polite to ask. She didn't even know how many she herself had. She'd lost count.

And she wasn't sure what the point of this conversation was. So she waited patiently for Maura to continue.

"Anyway, I asked Ms. Donahue, Ms. Winkle's assistant, about the files. She told me that Ms. Winkle checks each one every week. That's how she knows if a camper has enough demerits to get a warning."

Erin nodded. She knew the camp rule—if a girl got twenty-five demerits, her parents were sent a warning. And if she got fifty, she was sent home. But Erin didn't understand what all this had to do with Phyllis. Somehow, she didn't seem like the type who did things that got demerits. "Phyllis doesn't have a lot of demerits, does she?"

"Not *now*." Maura's smile grew even more conniving. "But she *could*."

Erin was confused. "I don't get it. Are you going to trick her into doing something that gets lots of demerits?"

"No, that's too much trouble," Andrea put in. "Maura's got a better idea."

Maura acknowledged the compliment with a

86

little nod. "And it's so simple! I'm surprised I didn't think of it ages ago."

The suspense was building. "Tell me!" Erin pleaded.

Suddenly, Maura was very serious. Her eyes, focused on Erin, were positively intense. "You're going to sneak into Ms. Winkle's cabin. You'll call up Phyllis's file on the computer. And then you'll add demerits to it. Enough to get rid of her for good."

A chill shot up Erin's spine. It rendered her speechless. She stared at Maura uncertainly, wondering if she could have misunderstood.

She hadn't. "See?" Maura asked. "It's perfect! Phyllis's parents are very strict. If they get a warning letter, they'll probably take her home even before Ms. Winkle orders them to. So you wouldn't even have to give her all that many demerits."

Somehow, Erin found her voice. "But—but maybe Phyllis doesn't have any demerits at all. Ms. Winkle will think it's very strange if all these demerits turn up on her file all of a sudden."

"Oh, c'mon," Andrea scoffed. "You know how Ms. Winkle is. She doesn't remember names, and half the time she gets one camper confused with another."

"Yeah," Ilene said. "I've been coming here for four years and she still calls me Denise."

What they were saying was true, and Erin knew it. Ms. Winkle ran a good camp, but she could get very spacey when it came to individual campers. That was probably why she kept such detailed files.

"You could do it tonight," Maura said.

"Tonight?" Erin's voice faltered.

"Sure, the sooner the better."

"The faster we get her out, the faster you can get in," Georgina added.

"Besides, it's the perfect time," Maura noted. "Everyone's here, and no one will notice if you slip away."

As her assignment sunk in, Erin sat very still. Then she gathered up all her courage and looked Maura in the eye. "But why do *I* have to do it? Why can't one of you?" Her eyes circled the group. Georgina was suddenly very interested in ripping a leaf. Denise was studying the stars.

Maura cocked her head to one side thoughtfully. "You want to be in our cabin, right?"

Erin nodded.

"Then you have to prove you've got what it takes to be a cabin nine girl. You have to show that you're worthy."

Erin considered this. "But I didn't tell on any

of you when I got caught at Camp Eagle. Doesn't that prove something?"

"That was good," Maura admitted. "But you have to remember that you're two years younger than us."

"One and a half," Erin corrected.

"Whatever. Anyway, we need to see that you're really committed and that you'll do the kind of things we do. Besides, you're the obvious person to do this. After all, you're the one who'll benefit when Phyllis leaves."

Now they were all watching her carefully, and Erin tried very hard not to let her apprehension show. This was a test. These were the coolest girls at camp. Now Erin had to prove she could be just as cool.

"Okay. But how am I going to get in? I know she leaves the main door open, but I think she locks her office door when she's not there."

"You can get in through a window," Andrea told her. "There's one that leads right into her office."

Erin gulped. This was even scarier than sneaking over to Camp Eagle.

Maura smiled kindly. "Why don't you go do it now and get it over with?"

Erin got up. At first, her legs felt stiff. Then they felt shaky. "All right."

Trying to look as inconspicuous as possible, she passed through the crowd, glancing behind every so often to make sure no one was watching. A few minutes later, she was standing outside Ms. Winkle's office. She could still hear the sounds coming from the camp fire area—faint laughter and conversation and some singing, too. But the camp fire seemed very far away. And she felt very alone.

She went up closer to the building and pressed her face against the window. The room was dark, but the light fixture on the outside of the building made it possible for her to see Ms. Winkle's desk. And right on top of the desk sat the computer.

From the shape of it, she thought it just might be the same kind her parents had at home. It probably wouldn't be difficult to figure out how to change the file.

Now she had to open the window. But maybe it would stick, and she wouldn't be able to budge it. The girls certainly wouldn't blame her if she couldn't get the window open. It wouldn't be her fault. But she had to give it a try.

Lightly, she tugged at it. It slid up smoothly, no problem at all. The window was low, and it was going to be very easy to climb in.

But she didn't. She just stood there, staring

at the open window. She still couldn't believe what she was about to do. Don't think about, she chided herself. Just get in there and do it.

But for some strange reason, her body didn't respond to her brain's command. She felt paralyzed.

"Erin."

The voice out of nowhere hit her like an electric shock. She whirled around. Katie was standing there, just a few feet away.

"Erin, what are you doing?"

Chapter 8

"What are you doing?" Katie asked again.

Erin was pretty sure there was guilt written all over her face. But she did her best to sound innocent. "Nothing."

As she expected, Katie looked extremely skeptical. "Sure, Erin. You opened that window. And you've been standing there staring at it for ages."

"How do you know I opened it?" Erin asked sharply.

"Because I followed you when you left the camp fire. And I've been watching you."

Erin glared at her. "What business do you have following me around?"

"I guess I'm worried about you."

"You're just nosy," Erin snapped. "And you're probably jealous because those older girls like me."

Katie groaned. "Give me a break. You think I want to hang around someone like Maura Kingsley? Or her creepy friend, Andrea? What I don't understand is why *you* want to be friends with *them.*"

"You don't even know them all that well," Erin replied.

"I know Maura well enough to know she pushes people around."

Erin had to laugh. "That's sort of like the pot calling the kettle black. Katie, you're the bossiest person I know."

Katie didn't appear offended by this. "Okay, maybe I can be bossy sometimes. But I don't try to force people to do bad things."

Erin stiffened. Had Katie been eavesdropping when Maura sent her on this mission? "What are you talking about?"

"That canoe trip to Eagle, for example."

"Maura didn't force me to do that. I wanted to go."

Katie actually grinned. "Yeah, and I'll bet you were scared stiff. I'll bet you wanted to come to Carolyn's party last night, too. But they probably talked you into staying there."

"No, they didn't," Erin said, but she could hear her own voice sounding feeble. Katie had a way of wearing a person down.

"What are they making you do now?"

Erin was about to claim nothing, but she knew it was useless. Here she stood, having just opened the window to Ms. Winkle's office. Obviously, she was getting ready to climb in. And obviously, she was about to do something she wasn't supposed to be doing.

She was caught, trapped, and Katie wouldn't leave her alone until she came up with a good story. But she couldn't think of one. And as she looked at Katie, she suddenly felt a desperate desire to confide in her. Even though she could predict exactly how Katie would react.

So she told her. Even as the words were leaving her mouth, she was amazed that she was telling her about it, because she knew there was no way Katie was going to let her go through with it. And at the same time, she realized that she really didn't want to go through with it anyway.

Katie's reaction was even stronger than Erin had anticipated. She couldn't remember ever seeing her look so shocked before.

"Erin, that's terrible! You can't do that!"

"I know," Erin murmured.

"It's wrong, it's worse than lying and stealing. And it's an awful thing to do to a person.

Especially someone like Phyllis. What did she ever do to you?"

"I know, I know," Erin repeated, louder this time. She plopped down on the ground and pulled her knees up, wrapping her arms around them. Katie paced in circles.

"It sounds like something Maura would think of. I can't believe you even considered doing it. See? I told you you were looking for trouble!"

"Oh, shut up," Erin growled. "I'm not in the mood for one of your lectures." She sighed heavily. "Now what am I going to do?"

"You're going to go right back there and tell Maura you won't do it."

"I *can't*," Erin wailed. "If I do that, they'll think I'm a jerk. They'll never speak to me again. They'll hate me."

"No, they won't. Well, maybe Maura and Andrea will. But I'd rather have them as enemies than friends anyway. Can't you see they're just using you?"

"Stop walking around me," Erin complained. "You're making me nervous."

Katie sat down next to her. "The rest of those kids won't hate you. Not if they're really your friends. In fact, they'll probably respect your decision."

Erin thought about Georgina, and Denise and

Ilene. They'd been so nice to her. She looked at Katie hopefully. "You really think so?"

"Absolutely."

Erin wished she could feel so confident. "Maybe I could just tell them I couldn't get the window open."

"They'll just find some other terrible thing for you to do. You better tell them the truth." She got up. "C'mon, let's go back to the camp fire."

Slowly, Erin rose. "Wait a minute." She went back to the window and closed it. Then they headed back to the camp fire area.

When they got closer, they separated. "Good luck," Katie whispered. Erin nodded grimly. She had a feeling she was going to need it.

The cabin nine girls looked up eagerly as she approached. Georgina gazed at her anxiously. "How'd it go?"

"Could you get in?" Denise asked.

Erin didn't sit down. She felt like she needed to be standing to say what she was about to say. "I didn't do it."

They were all startled. "Why not?" Andrea asked.

Erin took a deep breath. "Because—because I just couldn't. I'm sorry, but—"

Maura finished for her. "But you didn't have the guts."

"It's got nothing to do with guts. I just don't feel good about it. I mean, it's—it's wrong."

"So what?" Maura got up and faced her. "Look, Erin, grow up. Sometimes you have to do certain things to get what you want. Even if you think they're wrong."

"Maybe she's just not as mature as we thought she was," Andrea said in a snide way.

"Come on, Erin," Georgina wheedled. "Just go back and do it."

"I can't," Erin said miserably.

Maura's voice was hard and cold. "You have to."

Her words were like a slap in the face. Erin stepped back. "What do you mean, I have to. I don't *have* to do anything."

"Oh, yes you do." Maura moved in closer. "Because if you don't, we're going to Ms. Winkle and tell her you sneaked over to Camp Eagle Tuesday night."

Erin caught her breath. "But—but we all went."

"Yeah, but you were the only one who was seen. And we'll tell Ms. Winkle to ask Teddy about it." Her smile was so nasty it couldn't even be called a smile. "I'm sure he'll admit he found you. You'll be sent home. And I bet Teddy will be fired for not reporting you."

Erin was in a state of shock. She couldn't believe this. Maura was blackmailing her! She looked to Georgina, Denise, and Ilene, hoping one of them would say something. But they were looking at the ground, the stars, the fire—they were looking at everything but Erin.

"Uh-oh," Andrea said. "There goes Ms. Winkle."

Erin turned. The camp director was heading off with a couple of counselors in the direction of her office.

"They're probably having a meeting," Andrea groaned.

Well, that's that, Erin thought. There was no way she could get into the office now anyway.

But her sense of relief was short-lived. "You don't have to do it tonight," Maura said. "You've got till tomorrow night." She turned to Andrea. "Let's get something to eat."

The two of them strolled away. Erin sat down and faced the others. "What am I going to do?" There was no response.

"C'mon, you guys, it's awful to do something like that to a person, even a nerd like Phyllis! And you know it!"

The three cabin nine girls exchanged uncomfortable looks. Finally, Georgina spoke. "Look, Erin, we really like you. And maybe this is a pretty rotten thing to do to Phyllis. But we're not going to go against Maura. I mean, we stick together, you know?"

Erin knew. It was the same way in cabin six. Even if she had gone through that window tonight, with Katie watching, she knew her cabin mate wouldn't have reported her.

But there was a difference. Cabin six girls might not tell on each other. But that didn't mean they did nothing if they thought one of them was doing something wrong.

In a way, Katie was the leader in her cabin, just like Maura was the leader here. But the cabin six girls didn't follow Katie's every wish like little lambs. They argued and debated and sometimes did the opposite of what she wanted them to do. Because they were individuals. Not sheep.

Her eyes wandered from Georgina to Denise to Ilene. And even though they had great hair-dos and lots of style, she sort of felt sorry for them.

But not half as sorry as she felt for herself.

Chapter 9

In cabin six that night, the lights were out but no one was sleeping. The campers were all huddled on Trina's bed, listening in horror as Erin told them about Maura's threat.

"That's terrible!" Trina spoke in hushed tones, but her expression showed all the emotion she couldn't demonstrate in her voice.

Megan's face was stricken, too. "Erin, how could you hang around with such awful people?"

Erin shrugged. "They weren't all awful. Georgina's lots of fun. Denise and Ilene were nice, too."

"Don't defend them," Katie reproved her. "They didn't lift a finger to help when they heard Maura blackmail you."

"Yeah, that's true," Erin admitted sadly. "I guess Maura has that whole cabin under her control. And now she's got me under her thumb, too."

"Did you really sneak over to Camp Eagle at midnight?" Sarah asked in awe.

"Yeah. And we're all supposed to go over there again tomorrow night."

"But you're not going with them, are you?" Trina asked anxiously.

"I guess not."

Katie scowled. "How can you say you *guess* not? You sound like you *want* to go! How can you even consider it after the way they've treated you?"

"Oh, I'm not going," Erin assured her. "But I have to admit, it was sort of exciting."

"But what are you going to do about Maura?" Sarah asked. "If you don't put those demerits on the computer, and she does what she says she's going to do—"

"I know," Erin interrupted. She gestured helplessly. "I don't know what I'm going to do."

"The question is," Katie said, "what are *we* going to do?"

Erin raised her eyebrows. "What do you mean? It's not your problem."

"Yes, it is," Katie stated resolutely. "When one cabin six girl has a problem, all cabin six girls have a problem. You should know that by now, Erin."

"She's right," Trina said. "We'll think of a way to help you."

Megan nodded in agreement. "Cabin six girls always take care of each other."

"Always," Sarah echoed.

Erin gazed at them in amazement. Here she'd been practically ignoring them, treating them like dirt—and they were still willing to stick by her. She felt like crying. But she managed not to, since crying always left her eyes looking red and puffy and gross.

"Gee, you guys are really great."

"We know that," Sarah said smugly.

Erin grinned at her. "But I still think you should get contact lenses."

Katie frowned. "C'mon, get serious. We have to think. How are we going to get Erin out of this mess?"

The girls fell silent, each deep in her own thoughts. Megan yawned. Then Sarah yawned. It was contagious. Before long they were all yawning.

"I guess we're too tired to think of anything," Trina said. "We'd better sleep on it. Maybe we'll wake up with a brilliant scheme."

They separated and went to their own beds.

Erin was so exhausted she thought she'd fall asleep the minute her head hit the pillow. But she didn't. Her eyes remained wide open as she lay there and considered her options. She could add demerits to Phyllis's file. But she had an awful feeling that would stay on her conscience forever. Or she could refuse to do it, Maura would report her to Ms. Winkle, and her parents would be notified. She'd be sent home, and then she'd be grounded—forever. What a choice.

Then something distracted her. Katie sat up in bed. "I've got it!"

Erin leaped out of her bed. So did all the others. And once again, they converged on Trina's bed.

All traces of drowsiness had disappeared from Katie's eyes. They were bright and excited. "Erin, you've got one of those fancy cameras, right? The kind where the picture comes out right away?"

Erin nodded. "Yeah. So what?"

"Then I've got a brilliant scheme."

Erin's eyes widened in amazement and admiration as she listened to Katie's idea. The others had the same reaction. It was a pretty wild notion. But it just might work.

Only Trina looked a little troubled. "Doesn't

103

that mean we'd be doing the same kind of thing Maura's doing to Erin?"

Katie nodded. "Yeah, in a way. But in this situation, it's the only way." She narrowed her eyes grimly. "We're going to fight fire with fire."

Erin had just set her breakfast tray down on the table when Ilene appeared by her side. "Maura wants to see you."

It was like a summons. "Who is she, the Queen of England or something?" Sarah asked.

Erin could feel her cabin mates eyes on her as she followed Ilene to the cabin nine table. It didn't bother her this time, though. In a way, she felt supported.

The girls fell silent as she approached. Maura, as usual, took charge. "Have you decided what you're going to do, Erin?" Her voice was sugary.

Erin nodded. "I'll take care of it. Tonight."

Maura nodded in satisfaction. And Georgina looked pleased. "Don't forget, we're going to Eagle tonight."

"What time are you going?" Erin asked.

"We'll meet at the lake at midnight," Andrea said.

Erin pretended to be considering this. "Gee, I was thinking I'd better not try anything until midnight. You know, sometimes Ms. Winkle works in her office late. Maybe you guys better just go on without me."

"Oh well, we'll be going back again," Georgina said comfortingly.

"And the next time we go, you'll be going as a real cabin nine girl," Denise added.

Erin knew she was supposed to be thrilled by that notion. But all she could manage was a feeble grin. "I'd better get back to my table. I don't want them to get suspicious."

"Good idea," Maura said.

Erin hoped to avoid the cabin nine girls all day. It was hard facing them with Katie's scheme in her head. She wished she could get out of swimming. She wouldn't have to see them, plus she could preserve her French braid one more day. It was probably going to be the last one she'd have that summer. But Sarah wanted help with her diving, and Erin couldn't let her down again.

Luckily, the rest of the cabin six schedule that day didn't overlap with cabin nine's. And she managed to keep away from the cabin nine girls until just after dinner.

She had just left the dining hall with her cabin mates when Georgina caught up with her. "Erin, I have to talk to you." Reluctantly, Erin allowed Georgina to pull her away.

"I'm so glad you gave in," Georgina said. "I really want you in our cabin."

Erin nodded, but she kept her eyes on the ground. She was afraid that if she looked Georgina in the eye or said too much, she'd give everything away.

"Look, I understand how you feel about doing this to Phyllis," Georgina went on. "Just between us, I feel pretty crummy about it myself. When we were younger, Phyllis was just about my best friend at camp."

"Then why are you going along with Maura's plan?" Erin asked.

Georgina looked uncomfortable. "Well, you know how Maura is. She can come up with really nasty ideas. And Andrea always backs her up."

"But that's just two," Erin noted. "There's you, Denise, Ilene—and Phyllis. Why can't you stand up to her?"

Georgina shrugged. "It's just the way it is." Then she brightened. "Hey, maybe when you move in, we'll have the power to wear down some of her meanest schemes."

"You've already got the majority," Erin pointed out.

"Yeah, but . . ." Georgina's voice trailed off. Erin knew what the *but* was—but they didn't have the guts. And Erin knew that if she moved into cabin nine, nothing would change. She wasn't the type to pull them together in a rebellion. It would take someone a lot stronger than she was. Besides, if they hadn't rebelled by now, they never would.

"You know, you're actually doing Phyllis a favor," Georgina said. "She's got to be miserable here, the way we treat her. I gotta go. See you later!"

Erin nodded. She *would* be seeing Georgina later. But Georgina wouldn't be seeing her.

"Is Carolyn sleeping?" Katie asked in a whisper. Megan went over to the counselor's door and softly called, "Carolyn?" There was no response. "She's got to be asleep."

"I wish I was," Sarah mumbled drowsily.

"Not me," Megan said. "This is too exciting! I wish we could all go."

"Too risky," Katie said. "We might get seen. What time is it?"

"Quarter of twelve," Trina replied.

"Erin, are you sure there's film in the camera?" Katie asked.

"Positive." Erin hung the camera around her neck.

"Will it work at night?"

"Yeah, it's got one of those built-in lights."

Katie got up. "Okay. Let's go."

There was a chorus of hushed "good lucks" as Erin slowly opened the door, hoping it wouldn't creak and wake Carolyn. Then, without a word, she and Katie ran silently through the camp and down the bank toward the lake.

At that point, they began walking slowly and carefully to avoid any noises their footsteps might make. Finally, they came within sight of the canoes lying on the shore. Katie pointed wordlessly to a big rock, and Erin nodded. Together, they made their way to the rock and crouched behind it.

Erin leaned around the side of the rock and focused the camera to make sure they were in a good position. Then they stayed very still and waited.

Erin's legs were feeling cramped. She felt like hours were passing. But it was actually only a few minutes later when Katie whispered, "Here they come."

She didn't have to announce it. Erin could see them—Maura, Andrea, Georgina, Denise, and Ilene. They were coming down the bank. She could hear them, too, giggling and talking.

And for one brief moment, Erin remembered the night she'd been with them. Except for getting caught, it had been fun and exciting. But with all her willpower, she forced the memory from her mind.

The cabin nine girls began dragging the canoes toward the water. "Go," Katie hissed. Erin stuck her head out the side of the rock, aimed the camera, and hit the button. There was a buzzing sound, and then a photo emerged. Erin didn't bother to look at it. The photo would need a minute to develop into a real picture. Besides, she was too busy holding her breath and waiting to see if those girls had heard the buzz or seen the little flash of light.

But none of them was looking their way. They were busy wading into the water, dragging the canoes. There were faint shrieks of laughter as they climbed into them. Then they started rowing away, and Erin's camera clicked again.

Another photo came out. But still they stayed there behind the rock, motionless, until the canoes were too far away for their occupants to see them.

Katie grabbed the photos. "Let's go!" And they ran back up the bank.

Inside cabin six, the other girls, even Sarah, were wide awake. "What happened?" Megan asked eagerly. "Did it work?"

"Shh," Katie warned her, glancing at Carolyn's door. "Sarah, get your flashlight."

They all gathered on Trina's bed. Erin laid the two photos down, and Katie shined the flashlight on them.

A collective gasp came from the group. Katie grinned in triumph. "We've got them!"

Chapter 10

Erin knew they were watching her. Even with her back to them, she knew their eyes were on her.

Sarah confirmed this. She was sitting on the other side of the table, and she could see them. "They're all looking at you," she told Erin.

"I know," Erin said. But she wouldn't give them the satisfaction of turning around in her seat. She poured some milk into her cereal bowl.

"When are we going to do it?" Megan asked. She was bouncing in her seat. Erin was on the verge of telling her she was acting like a baby, but she thought better of it. She was going to need all the friends she could get.

"We're not doing anything yet," Katie said. "No one's going to say *we* started anything. Let them make the first move."

"Hey, wait a minute," Erin objected. "It's me

who's in trouble here. I think I should be making that decision."

"Okay," Katie said agreeably. "What do you think we should do?"

Erin thought it over. "Let's let them make the first move."

"Excellent idea," Katie said.

Carolyn joined them at the table. She smiled at them all, but her smile lingered longer on Erin. "I'm glad you're sitting with us again. It's nice having you back." She wasn't being sarcastic, the way Katie had been. Her voice was sincere.

Erin smiled back. "Yeah, well, I'll probably be sitting here from now on."

"Really?" Carolyn took a piece of toast. "What about your other friends?"

Megan immediately started giggling, Sarah started coughing, and Erin shot them both a warning look. Carolyn's eyes darted around the table.

"Is there something going on I'm not aware of?"

Katie nodded. "No offense, Carolyn, but it's kind of a secret."

"Oh." Carolyn reached for the butter. "I understand."

She didn't sound the least bit hurt. That was

something really nice about Carolyn, Erin thought. She accepted the fact that they had secrets they couldn't share with her. She wasn't really like a baby-sitter at all, no matter what Maura said.

Across from Erin, Trina went a little pale. "Uh-oh. Here comes one of them."

It was Georgina this time. She smiled brightly at Erin. "Hi! Can you come over to our table? Maura wants to ask you something." Her tone was casual, and Erin could tell that was for Carolyn's sake.

Erin glanced quickly at Katie and then turned back to Georgina. "I'm eating right now. Why don't you tell her I'll meet her right after breakfast, outside."

Georgina blinked. "But she wants to see you now."

Erin flipped her hair over her shoulder and smiled. "She can wait till after breakfast."

Georgina was taken aback. Then she spoke hesitantly. "Well, okay. I'll tell her."

Sarah watched her walk back to her table. "Are those girls her slaves or what?"

Katie winked at Erin. "You handled that really well."

"Thank you." Erin had an enormous urge to turn around and catch Maura's expression when she got Georgina's message. But she was afraid it might totally freak her out.

The cabin six table was unusually quiet for the rest of the meal. Erin figured they were all feeling what she was feeling—a little excited, a little nervous, and a little afraid of saying anything for fear of spilling the beans in front of Carolyn.

Carolyn had to know something was going on. She'd be a total space cadet if she didn't. But she didn't say a word.

Erin dawdled over breakfast. She wanted to put the confrontation off as long as possible. But finally, Carolyn got up. "You girls go on back to the cabin and straighten up, okay? I've got a short counselors' meeting here, and then I'll be back." She left to go to another table where counselors had gathered.

"Look," Trina said. Erin turned. Over at the cabin nine table, the girls were getting up. Maura caught her eye. She cocked her head toward the exit. Erin nodded.

Katie was observing this too. "Okay, let's go meet them."

"You guys don't have to come with me," Erin said bravely. "I can handle this."

"We wouldn't let you face them alone," Sarah replied. "United we stand and all that."

"That's right." Megan lowered her voice to a growl. "If you mess with one cabin six girl, you mess with all of them." She sounded like a gangster. Erin would have laughed if she wasn't feeling slightly sick. But it was definitely going to make everything easier with them by her side. Together, they rose, returned their trays, and walked to the exit.

Maura and the others were waiting just outside the door. They looked surprised when they saw all the cabin six girls approach them.

Maura folded her arms across her chest. "Erin, we want to talk to you privately."

Erin gathered up every ounce of courage she had and stepped forward. "I don't have any secrets from my cabin mates."

The five mouths facing her dropped open. Maura was the first to recover from this announcement. "Are you *sure* about that, Erin?"

"Positive."

Maura gestured nonchalantly. "All we want to know is whether or not you took care of that little business we talked about."

Erin swallowed. Then, somehow, she got the word out. "No."

A dead silence fell over the group. Then Katie spoke. "Is something wrong with your mouths? Or do they just naturally hang open like that?"

115

"Very funny, Katie," Maura snapped. "This is all none of your business, you know."

"Oh, yes it is," Katie declared. "You can't blackmail a cabin six girl and get away with it so easily."

Georgina gasped. "Erin—you told them about Eagle?"

Erin nodded. "I told them everything. And they're not going to let you guys get me sent home."

Maura raised her eyebrows. "Oh, no?" She turned to the others. "I think we should go see Ms. Winkle." She turned as if to go back inside.

"Wait a minute!" Erin called. Maura stopped, turned back, and smiled. "Are you having second thoughts?"

"No. But I've got something to show you." Erin reached into her pocket and withdrew the photos. Puzzled, Maura reached out for them, but Erin held them back.

"You can't have them. But you can look at them."

The cabin nine girls gathered around her. And as they examined the photos, their mouths fell open again. Mentally, Erin thanked her parents for getting her one of the more expensive instant-picture cameras. The photos had come out really well. Each girl was recognizable, and it was very obvious what they were doing.

"Why, you little sneak!" Maura burst out.

"Erin!" Georgina wailed. "How could you do that?"

The others didn't say anything. They just stared at the photos with shocked and stunned expressions.

"You guys still want to go see Ms. Winkle?" Katie asked sweetly. "Maybe we'll go with you."

Maura appeared to be too furious to speak. Next to her, Denise looked frightened. "You're not really going to show those to Ms. Winkle, are you, Erin?" she asked in a small voice.

Erin put the photos back in her pocket. "I guess we could make a deal."

Maura glared at her. But Erin figured she was smart enough to know when the game was over.

"We better get back to the cabin," Andrea murmured.

Maura nodded. "Yeah. C'mon, you guys."

Obediently, they followed her. No one said good-bye, not even Georgina. But over her shoulder, Maura threw one last parting shot at Erin. "And we thought you were *mature*. Boy, were we wrong!"

The cabin six girls watched them retreat in silence. Then they burst into cheers. Katie

117

hugged Erin, Megan hugged Trina, and finally they just made one big group hug. That was the position they were in when Carolyn came outside.

"Hey, what's all this?" she asked, grinning. "You guys are supposed to be making beds, not hugging."

"We just *love* each other," Megan squealed.

Erin rolled her eyes. They were all acting like idiots, like babies. But for once, she didn't care.

As they headed back to the cabin, she turned to Carolyn. "You were right."

"About what?" Carolyn asked.

"About knowing who my real friends are."

Carolyn put an arm around her shoulder. "I had a feeling you'd find that out."

Off in the distance, Erin could still see the cabin nine girls. And despite all that had happened, she still felt a little wistful. It had been nice, being with girls who cared about things like hairstyles and makeup and boys. It might have been fun, living in cabin nine.

But then she looked around at the girls walking with her. And she decided that cabin six wasn't such a bad place to be. At least she had friends she could count on there.

Even if they *were* immature.

MEET THE GIRLS FROM CABIN SIX IN

CAMP SUNNYSIDE FRIENDS

Coming Soon

CAMP SUNNYSIDE FRIENDS #5
LOOKING FOR TROUBLE

75909-8 ($2.50 US/$2.95 Can)

When the older girls at camp ask Erin to join them in some slightly-against-the-rules escapades, she has to choose between appearing cool and being mature.

Don't Miss These Other
Camp Sunnyside Adventures:

(#4) NEW GIRL IN CABIN SIX
75703-6 ($2.50 US/$2.95 Can)

(#3) COLOR WAR!   75702-8 ($2.50 US/$2.95 Can)

(#2) CABIN SIX PLAYS CUPID
75701-X ($2.50 US/$2.95 Can)

(#1) NO BOYS ALLOWED!   75700-1 ($2.50 US/$2.95 Can)

HOWLING GOOD FUN
FROM AVON CAMELOT

Meet the 5th graders of P.S. 13—
the craziest, creepiest kids ever!

M IS FOR MONSTER
　　　　　75423-1/$2.75 US/$3.25 CAN
by Mel Gilden; illustrated by John Pierard

BORN TO HOWL　　75425-8/$2.50 US/$3.25 CAN
by Mel Gilden; illustrated by John Pierard

THERE'S A BATWING IN MY
　　LUNCHBOX　　75426-6/$2.75 US/$3.25 CAN
by Ann Hodgman; illustrated by John Pierard

THE PET OF FRANKENSTEIN
　　　　　75185-2/$2.50 US/$2.50 US/$3.25 CAN
by Mel Gilden; illustrated by John Pierard

Z IS FOR ZOMBIE　75686-2/$2.75 US/$3.25 CAN
by Mel Gilden; illustrated by John Pierard

MONSTER MASHERS
　　　　　75785-0/$2.75 US/$3.25 CAN
by Mel Gilden; illustrated by John Pierard